PUFFIN STORY BOOKS

Edited by Eleanor Graham

PS106

STORM AHEAD

This is a magnificent story of action and suspense. Most of it happens in one weekend – a weekend when time stood still for the Marsh folk, including Rissa and Tamzin, Roger and Meryon (see *The White Riders*). Out of a warm November day when the sun felt like high summer, came disaster – gale, storm, flood. As Jim Decks the ferryman said to Rissa, 'Tidn't nacheral, choose how! Stands to reason you gotter pay for them frolics, see?' They paid. Maroons called out the lifeboat, and everyone in the village came forward to help. In a moment of light Roger saw that 'the tide was high above the highest mark they had ever known it reach before, and the whole sea under the white moonlight was a range of towering, melting mountains, white-topped as any other peaks, but terrifyingly mobile' – and the lifeboat was out in it. The suspense is tremendous, but so truly based that the whole great story reads like something actually experienced and lived through. It is real life, and told with the responsibility felt in any great emergency when all possible help is needed and even children do the right thing as though inspired. Boys and girls (probably over 10 or 11) and grownups will surely enjoy it equally. It would be grand for reading aloud.

MONICA EDWARDS

STORM AHEAD

With illustrations by Geoffrey Whittam

PENGUIN BOOKS

Penguin Books Ltd, Harmondsworth, Middlesex
U.S.A.: Penguin Books Inc., 3300 Clipper Mill Road, Baltimore 11, Md
CANADA: Penguin Books (Canada) Ltd, 178 Norseman Street,
Toronto 18, Ontario
AUSTRALIA: Penguin Books Pty Ltd, 762 Whitehorse Road,
Mitcham, Victoria

—

First published by Collins 1953
Published in Puffin Story Books 1957

Made and printed in Great Britain
by C. Nicholls & Company Ltd

CONTENTS

ILLUSTRATIONS

CHAPTER I

QUITE PECULIAR

*

LINDSEY THORNTON recognized Tamzin before the train had properly pulled up in Dunsford station. This was not a difficult thing to do as Tamzin was almost the only person waiting on the platform this quiet and strangely warm November midday, when the sun shone as if it were high summer. She had seen Lindsey, too, and was running along the platform to be level with her carriage when it stopped.

'Hallo, you!'

'Hallo, yourself! I must have come to the right place, as the right person's on the platform.'

Tamzin grinned. 'Didn't you expect to? Here, let me heave one of those suitcases.'

Lindsey was on the platform, glancing back to thank a lean Marshman who helped her with her luggage.

'I suppose it was more hoping to, than expecting to,' she said, turning to follow Tamzin down the platform as the doors banged shut along the train. 'It's the first time I've ever travelled so far alone, and there were two changes.'

'Not bad for thirteen,' Tamzin grinned.

'As if you weren't thirteen yourself!'

The train was creaking and fussing out of the station again and Tamzin led the way cautiously over the crossing. 'Only till next month. My birthday's at Christmas, of all the unlikely times.'

'Oh, too bad! Half a minute, while I excavate my ticket.'

They dumped the cases on the dusty platform and Lindsey groped in her pocket for the ticket. Anyone watching them might easily have taken them for sisters, if only because of the long swinging plaits, grey eyes, and fair complexions. But Lindsey, though nearly a year the younger, was quite as tall as Tamzin; she was heavier and her plaits were longer and browner than Tamzin's tawny ones.

'Here it is; no, that's the return half. This is it. Have you got the pony-trap outside? I rather hoped you'd have Rissa and young Diccon with you, too.'

Tamzin handed in her platform ticket and moved on through the gateway.

'No, not the pony-trap, and not Diccon; you haven't got a very small brother, or you wouldn't ask! But Rissa's somewhere around.'

They were both out now, at the bottom of the broad hill that led from the station to the high little town that was as old as British history.

'Not the trap?' Lindsey was surprised and disappointed, following Tamzin up the hill beside the cattle market. 'Oh, Tamzin! You don't mean you've plumped for the bus or anything humdrum like that? Is that Rissa over there?'

Tamzin gave a high snort of delighted laughter. 'That? Rissa? If only she'd heard you say so! Hat, coat, and gloves – and in this weather!'

'Well, it is November, even if it does feel like August. There's a bus that says Westling, over there.'

'It'd all be the same to Rissa if it was January. And we don't have to bother about the bus; I've got a better plan. Pity these cases are so heavy though – I'd forgotten about them – because we have to heave them along at least two or three hundred yards yet.'

'It's because Mother would put piles of apples and

butter and cream and things in them. I said they were rather dull for presents, but she said she thought they wouldn't be to anyone who didn't live on a farm.'

'She was jolly well right!' said Tamzin decisively. 'Especially about the cream. One thing about Westling is that it isn't a very cow-ish place, being almost all shingle and saltings. Well, there are cows, of course, that the Deeproses keep at Harbour Farm, but not enough for selling cream or anything; just the milk for the village.'

They rounded the corner where the station hill turned into Cinque Ports Street and headed out towards the river and the Strand. But after a few more yards they dumped the cases for the relief of aching arms and fingers, and stared into the wide windows of Gasson's Marine Stores as they rested.

'Lovely shop,' said Lindsey, pressing her nose against the glass. 'Nothing like this in Godalming. Look at those ships' lanterns, against the pile of netting.'

Tamzin was flexing stiff fingers.

'It doesn't only look nice from outside,' she said, 'it smells nice inside, too. You know – oilskins and rope and tarred string, and that rough wool the navy guernseys are made from. But we haven't time now, with Rissa waiting.' She bent to pick up the suitcase. 'Come on! That shop's a lot older than we are; it'll still be there when we come back – or when you come back, I suppose I should say, as I'll be at school, worse luck, except for week-ends.'

Lindsey said, 'I don't know that you're right about the worse luck part: not if you mean worse than mine. It wasn't much fun having measles with complications, and that's the only reason I'm here instead of at my school. I say! A little harbour! Look, Tamzin!'

Lindsey stopped dead in sudden surprised admiration

as they reached the place where the road swept broadly round on to the wide Strand flanking the tidal river at the skirts of the steeply hilly town. The masts of yachts and fishing-boats were like a little winter forest in the unseasonably warm November sunlight, and the dinghies gently pulled against their painters, swinging seawards with the gliding of the water.

'Oh, look!' said Lindsey, absorbing every detail with the sudden awareness of surprise.

Tamzin had not stopped.

'Yes, I know,' she said over her shoulder. 'But it's our own harbour at Westling that I specially love. Wait till you see that! It isn't so old as this, but it looks much older; perhaps partly because there's much more timber and less concrete about it, and more fishing boats than up here. Oh look, there's old Rissa; in the big black dinghy astern of the green yacht. She'll come down to Westling with us and stay for tea, but she lives here in Dunsford, of course. And you remember me telling you about Meryon and Roger?'

'Roger was Rissa's cousin, or something?'

'Yes, and lives in Hastings. But he's often at Meryon's house in Winklesea. Well, they're probably coming to tea as well, because Roger's down for half-term. We shan't see them till tea-time, though, as they'll be coming over the Marsh.'

Lindsey screwed up her eyes against the westering sun as they walked on down to the river, their shoulders leaning outwards to take the weight of the suitcases. She said, 'If sailing home down the river was your plan it certainly *is* a much better one than the bus! Even than the pony-trap for me, because the one thing we don't get at Punchbowl Farm is anything at all to do with boats.'

'That's what I thought,' said Tamzin, changing

hands on her suitcase, 'only it won't be sailing because there absolutely isn't a breath of wind – oddly enough, for these parts; we're generally blown almost off the earth. But when we realized the tide would be just right for going down with it, we borrowed the smack's punt from Walter Goddard – he's one of the fishermen – and sculled up on the last of the flood.'

'It's going out pretty fast now, isn't it?' Lindsey said, as they came down to the river's edge and turned along the wharf.

'Oh yes; we can drift down with hardly any work at all. Rissa's seen us.' Tamzin lifted the hand that wasn't gripping the suitcase and the navy-jerseyed figure in the black punt waved in reply. 'She did a bit of shopping while I went down to the station: some sausages for old Jim – he's the ferryman and the nicest, wickedest person you can think of – and some navy wool to finish a guernsey he's knitting.'

'What? *Knitting*, did you say? Oh, doesn't that old red town look sort of magical from here! All scrambling up its hill.'

'Yes. And I did say knitting. They all do it; it's quite commonplace in Westling. They knit socks too. I suppose it comes of being long hours at sea, and they don't think it's a bit sissy. Hallo, Rissa! This is Lindsey.'

They were standing on the edge of the wharf directly above the smack's punt, which Rissa was manoeuvring in to an iron ladder rising abruptly from the high water to the wharf. She glanced up over her shoulder and smiled briefly.

'Hallo! You're the one she met stalking in Surrey bracken!'

'The one,' agreed Lindsey, watching her bring the punt's broad stern round, ship the single oar and turn to grasp the iron ladder. Now Rissa looked up squarely and smiled a proper greeting. She was like an ancient Egyptian, Lindsey thought suddenly; like a pharaoh's daughter, with her gipsy-dark skin and her thick straight hair swinging heavily just above her shoulders.

'You go down first,' Tamzin said to Lindsey, 'and I'll hand you the loot.'

Lindsey screwed herself round, feeling with her foot for the first rung, then down she went, still screwed round because the high water held the boat only a few rungs lower than the top of the ladder. The big punt scarcely rocked as she stepped into it and turned to reach up for the cases.

'Stow them up in the bows,' Rissa said, her hand still on the ladder as Tamzin came hopping down it, 'unless they're very heavy. If they are we'll have to have one amidships.'

'They're not as heavy as that,' said Tamzin, stepping down into the boat. 'Push off, Rissa. Don't let's lose any of the tide.'

Rissa pushed off with her hand, then with the oar braced against the concrete wall. The black punt nosed into midstream and began to glide down river as Tamzin and Lindsey stowed the luggage and dumped themselves down upon the centre thwart.

'I always thought,' said Lindsey, as they glided smoothly between the moored vessels in the harbour, 'that a punt was a sort of fancy, narrow boat you shove along fashionable rivers with a pole.'

Rissa was steering with her single oar over the stern.

'Nearly everyone thinks that,' she said, 'unless they've lived in fishing villages.'

'Down here,' said Tamzin, staring curiously at a strange trawler, 'they are smack's dinghies. Bigger than ordinary dinghies.'

'And much, much dirtier!' grinned Rissa.

16

'A thousand times dirtier than fashionable punts!'
said Tamzin, laughing. She tossed overboard a small
withered flatfish from the bottom of the boat and
scraped with her heel against the coating of dried fish-
scales on the boards.

'Yes, thank goodness!' agreed Rissa. 'I like 'em
dirty. Nice rich, tarry-fishy-bilgy smell that sticks to
your hands and all your clothes and reminds you of the
river and the sea when you're marooned at home with
nothing to save you from your homework.'

She was sculling slowly over the stern

The flatfish was so shrivelled that it floated for a
while, like a bit of old shoe-leather, then lost itself in the
milky swirl of Rissa's sculling and disappeared beneath
the blackness of the river.

Rissa was standing, now, her feet planted squarely

astride and her back to Tamzin and Lindsey. She was sculling slowly over the stern, the long oar resting in a groove cut out specially for it. Her hands swept smoothly from side to side with a practised twist of the wrists, the shining blade describing bright arcs in the water as it drove the boat steadily downstream. Their speed seemed out of all proportion to Rissa's leisurely movements, because they had the current with them. The punt rocked gently in time to the sweeping of the oar and Tamzin and Lindsey rocked gently with the punt. Rissa herself swayed loosely from the hips as she sculled, like a metronome keeping time to a largo. Her long square bob swung heavily in the windless air.

'I hope you won't be awfully bored,' Tamzin was saying, 'with Rissa and me at school for most of the time. It isn't even as if we had light evenings.'

'It doesn't look the sort of place where any right-minded person could be bored, even alone,' Lindsey said. 'I could spend hours just messing about this wharf, watching those men mending nets, and that one painting the houseboat, and those people unloading timber from the barge.'

'Then you'll like it even better, messing around our harbour,' said Tamzin. She was leaning over the side, brown fingers raking the water till they caught and lifted up a lump of cork floating slowly down the river. 'Diccon wanted some to float his soap on, in the bath.'

'He's her small brother,' Rissa explained.

'I know,' said Lindsey. 'He collects snails.'

'And slugs – and spiders,' said Tamzin, 'and all kinds of other low life.' She shook the cork and the dark river water, suddenly turned to crystal in the sunlight, showered brilliantly outwards. It ran down Tamzin's wrist and, when she stowed the cork beneath the thwart, it spread in a round wet smudge upon the boards. She wiped her palm up and down her navy jersey sleeve, turning her hand to dry the back of it, and the fine dark fibres of the wool clung damply to her skin, leaving it as hairy-looking as any Westling fisherman's.

Lindsey said, 'Speaking of being bored – what weather! It's just as hot as summer.'

'Jim didn't like it much when we saw him in the morning,' Tamzin said.

'Not like it? Do they have to have it rough for fishing?'

'He said it wouldn't last. Said it was the kind of calm that hatched a hurricane.'

'What, here?' Lindsey said disbelievingly.

Rissa screwed her shoulders to check her direction as they swung round the bend below the shipyard.

'I expect he meant,' she said, 'that he'd seen it hatch a hurricane in the places where you get them. But we can get a snorter even here.' She was sculling with a wide smooth stroke again and facing to the stern, her words drifting patchily over her shoulders as she swayed. 'I live in Dunsford, of course, so I don't get the full whack of it; but there's nothing at all between the sea and Westling Vicarage, except a mile or so of saltings, so Tamzin gets the lot. They even have double windows on all one side of their house.'

Tamzin said thoughtfully, 'It's awful cleaning them. But Mother pays extra for the double ones, so there is something to be got out of them – Hard a-port, Rissa! Another yard and we'd have been sitting on the mud.'

Rissa swung the punt into the stream again.

'The river bends sharper here than you'd think it does.'

Tamzin said, 'I don't see why you're sculling at all, with this tide. We're going a great lick anyhow.'

'Oh well,' said Rissa, sitting down again. She held

the oar like a tiller, keeping the punt straight. 'The only thing is, if Jim was really right about the weather it might be best to get a move on.'

Lindsey looked up and out over the vast sky that arched above the Marsh and sea. Landwards, the steep hill on which the little town was built stood high into the blue.

'There isn't a cloud. There isn't even a breath.'

'But there is a cloud,' said Tamzin suddenly, nodding seawards.

Rissa and Lindsey looked.

'Are you sure it isn't haze? It's very low,' said Rissa.

'It's a cloud,' Tamzin said. 'I'm sure.' She began to strip off her heavy jersey, which she wore over a summer aertex shirt. 'Gosh!' she said. 'I wish there was a breath, too. The heat!'

'It's almost silly, isn't it, for November?' Lindsey grinned, and her coat joined Tamzin's jersey in the bows.

'There are even boys swimming,' said Rissa, looking down the river. 'Of course, we have ourselves in November, I know; but only in a sort of bravado, when we were younger.'

'Those boys are swimming because they like it, you can see,' said Lindsey. 'I jolly well wish I'd brought my own swim-suit. Not that anyone would have thought of needing such a thing, at this time of year.'

'Anyway, I expect the water's cold,' said Tamzin consolingly.

They drifted on round the foot of the old town, down the Rock Channel, past the shouting, splashing swimmers, past the South Undercliff and out to where the river forked sharply, turning back to head across the open saltings and the Marsh towards the sea. The high, red town slowly receded and the great sky widened all around the gliding punt. Lindsey was looking at it again, fascinated.

'I suppose the sky's really the same everywhere, but it's funny how absolutely *enormous* your sky looks to me, after years of living in a valley and only seeing the sky as a long, narrow strip. Except when we go up on to the high fields, of course, and then I feel the same as here.'

'It's the same,' said Rissa, 'when you live in a town; even a little town like Dunsford. The sky is all chopped about with roofs and chimneys and trees and things, and then suddenly you come out into this.'

'"A hundred square miles without a shadow,"' quoted Tamzin. Then, 'It is a cloud.'

Lindsey and Rissa looked again, squinting into the brightness.

'So it is,' said Rissa.

'Funny colour, too,' said Lindsey.

'It's nearer,' Tamzin said.

'Not much,' said Rissa, 'but it is a funny colour.'

'Orange,' said Lindsey.

'Not absolutely orange,' said Tamzin. 'Perhaps a pinky orange, and a bit olive green.'

The punt drifted on, and now Lindsey was steering, sometimes practising the twisty sculling stroke but not with much success.

'You dig too deeply, I think,' Rissa told her.

'It's like swimming, or milking,' Tamzin said. 'Difficult at first, and then suddenly it comes easily.'

'Like rising to the trot,' said Lindsey.

'Or walking on your hands,' said Rissa.

'Or riding a bicycle,' said Tamzin.

Rissa turned to watch the sculling.

'You should make a sort of figure-of-eight in the water. Wider than that, and not so deep. That's better.

And twist your wrists so that the blade cuts through the water.'

'Oh,' said Lindsey suddenly. 'Like this!'

But then, after a few powerful, clean strokes, she was digging deeply again and nearly losing the oar.

'Did you feel that?' Tamzin had turned her face back towards the north.

'No, what?' Lindsey was too absorbed in her sculling.

'A puff of wind,' Rissa said. 'Only a puff, but it was nice while it lasted. Cool.'

'It was *cold*,' Tamzin said. 'Funny, really, in all this heat-wave weather. And that wasn't the only funny thing about it, either,' she suddenly added. 'It came from the north.'

'Cold winds usually do,' said Rissa sensibly.

'Yes, but the pinky cloud is coming from the south.'

'Thunder, I expect,' said Lindsey. 'At least, that's what we usually get with clouds travelling against the wind. D'you want to scull now, Tamzin?'

'Don't let's any of us scull,' said Rissa. 'It's too hot.'

But Tamzin took the oar. 'You were the one who suggested getting a move on,' she said. 'Not that I think the storm will beat us home, but I wouldn't mind wagering my share of Lindsey's cream that there's going to be one. For one thing, look at the sheep.'

'They do look uneasy,' Lindsey said, 'huddling up like that, and not grazing or anything.'

'I've never known Jim wrong about the weather,' Rissa admitted. Suddenly there was another cold breath.

'That one was from a different direction,' said Tamzin.

'Like a cold slap,' Lindsey said. 'Gone as soon as it comes, and leaving the air just as stifling. Do you often get such queer weather on the Marsh?'

Tamzin was sculling a little stronger now and rocking the boat with her movement. She paused a moment, her oar out astern like a rudder, and sniffed the stuffy air.

'No, I don't think I remember anything at all, ever, just like this. Usually we get a downright bluster, and no funny business whatever. I mean, with ordinary Marsh weather it's like living with someone who has a terribly wild temper but doesn't really mean any harm. This weather, now, is like – well, like someone plotting something out.'

'And of course,' said Rissa, 'it's very odd to have no wind at all. Wind is the one thing we pretty well always have around here. I should say you could count on one-and-a-half fingers the days in the year that have no wind whatever.'

'On half a finger,' corrected Tamzin, 'if even that.'

'I suppose that's why the few trees you have are all leaning over so far,' said Lindsey. Her chin was propped in her cupped hands, her elbows on her knees, and her brown plaits swung slowly to the rocking of the boat.

The water scarcely rippled at the punt's bows as she slid on down the smooth river that lay like a band of dull grey silk. The sun was low, huge and copper-coloured, and the smoke from Westling cottage chimneys hung heavy over the red roofs, flopping downwards as if with exhaustion from struggling out into the daylight.

After a while Lindsey suddenly said, 'The worst thing that happened to me after measles was my ears. I expect I have weak ones or something, but when everyone else gets germs in their throats or chests or noses I get them in the ears.'

Tamzin and Rissa made sympathetic noises and Lindsey went on, 'Well . . . what's worrying me a bit

23

now is that both my ears are feeling most extraordinary. I should hate to have all that fuss and bother again while I'm being a guest – I mean, not from my point of view, of course, but from Mrs Grey's and everyone's.' She frowned in her anxiety, her head held a little on one side as if the better to judge the symptoms.

Rissa, who had been tying knots in a length of tarry rope, looked up with a sudden grin.

'And to think,' she said, 'that at just the moment you spoke I was about to say, "Do anyone else's ears feel funny?" Because mine are quite peculiar.'

Lindsey's face cleared in sudden relief and Tamzin began laughing as she sculled.

'Mine are *popping*!' she said. 'What a very queer coincidence!'

'It isn't a coincidence,' said Rissa. 'I'll tell you what it is. It's the weather.' She dropped the tarry rope back into the bottom of the boat and yawned terrifically. 'Don't do that, either of you,' she grinned, stopping in the middle and swallowing the remnants of the yawn. 'It makes them feel even funnier. I'll have a go at that oar now, Tamzin, shall I? My, but if only we could get a breath of *air*.'

Even as she spoke, the chill squall hit them, pouncing from the east with the lightning fury of a tiger's unexpected leap. The little boat heeled over on her side, the coat and jerseys in the bows were sucked up in the wind and whisked away.

'Too late!' said Rissa, shouting into the sudden scream of the squall as she flung herself forward after them, her hands closing on empty air.

'All our things!' said Tamzin, frantically hanging on to the oar while crouching in the stern. 'Lie down, Lindsey! In the bottom of the boat. Don't be an ass, Rissa; get down!'

Rissa had rescued the sausages and knitting wool from where they rolled upon the tilted side of the boat, and she was climbing over the centre thwart to stow them down between the cases in the bows.

'Another minute and we'll be aground,' she said cheerfully, her thick hair streaming from her head, her knuckles white against the brown skin of her hands from the strain of their grip upon the thwart.

Then suddenly the squall had gone.

Profound quiet was around them again. The little boat swung slowly back to an even keel and was sliding once more towards the Harbour.

'Well!' said Tamzin, raising herself cautiously, first her head and then the rest of her.

'At least you still have the oar,' said Lindsey. She was kneeling now, in all the scales and slime and upon the burst remains of one of Jim Decks's sausages. 'Do you suppose that was the storm?'

'I shouldn't think so,' Tamzin said. 'I should think it was just the beginning. I say, Rissa, it does rather seem as if we oughtn't to waste time, but what about the coat and jerseys?'

Rissa glanced up and around.

'Well, it doesn't look too bad, and they may be fairly handy: it was only a very short gust. Let's have a go at finding them. We shan't be very popular if we walk in without them.'

'Oh well . . . all right.' Tamzin turned the boat's nose in to the bank with two sweeping strokes of her oar. 'I must say, I think this is the oddest weather. You could light a match this minute and I don't believe the flame would even flicker.'

'There's a good landing place,' Rissa pointed.

'Did the things land in the river? Did anyone see?' asked Tamzin, nosing in.

'They aren't floating anywhere,' said Lindsey.

'Pity they're all navy and dark brown. Much harder to see,' said Rissa.

Tamzin gave one more twist to the oar and then shipped it. The boat grounded on the submerged edge of the grazings and Rissa jumped out with the painter.

They were nearly twenty minutes in finding the lost garments, then found them all quite close together where a flock of sheep had huddled in the squall. They appeared undamaged, except for muddy hoof-marks, and were thankfully carried back to the grounded boat. There had been no more squalls during their search. Only another of those strange cold breaths, this time from the north again, but the air was even more heavily oppressive than before, and the orange-pinky cloud now fanned above the sea's rim in its slow progress up the sky.

The boat was pushed off the bank and Lindsey and Tamzin climbed in to stow the clothes again: then Rissa shoved clear with the long oar, and they were heading for Westling Harbour. The village was much nearer now, the houses and shipping starkly silhouetted against the low sun and the glowing, spreading cloud. Tamzin, looking at it all over her shoulder, suddenly said, 'Rissa, do you see what I see?'

'Mm?' Rissa narrowed her eyes towards the Harbour. 'Gosh, yes! Lindsey, see the Harbour Mast? That very tall one, there between the houses? See the little black cone-shaped thing swinging from it? That's the storm cone. They must have had a gale warning.'

'But I should think,' said Lindsey dryly, 'that everyone in these parts knew it already, long ago.'

CHAPTER 2

INTO THE STORM'S PATH

*

OLD Jim Decks was down at the water's edge waiting for them as they sculled in. The sky had darkened, the sun gone altogether under the advance of the swelling cloud, which now was more black than orange. Still there was that sinister airlessness, almost as if the whole village were enclosed within a low-ceilinged room in which all doors and windows had been shut for many years.

The boat ran into the shingle bank below the ferry hut and old Jim laid his hard hands on it as Tamzin jumped out with the painter.

'Gi' us that, gal, and I'll make 'er fast fer the night. Be a rough un. I toldjer that this morning, didn't I? Now I'll lay you can see it a-coming fer yerselves.'

Lindsey climbed out with one of her cases and Rissa followed with the other and the sausages and knitting wool.

'Here you are, Jim, and here's the change. So they've run the storm cone up.'

'Ah, fer a southerly gale. Shoulda done it afore, with the glass gorn down pr' nigh a inch since morning. Makes yer ears go wambly, that low, and it ent often that happens in this latitude, choose how.' He pocketed the coins Rissa gave him and tucked the parcels underneath his arm. 'Now I can git on with me guernsey. Time enough, too, fer this one fare to be proper wore out.'

'All our ears have been very odd,' said Tamzin,

pressing her left one gently with an experimental finger.

'Ah. That's low pressure, that is. Never knowed the glass so low, not in these parts. We got it coming, sure enough. And the spring tides, too; you couldn't have it wuss.'

They were walking up the shingle path to the ferry hut, and the old man's thick white hair and beard were startling in their radiance against the blackness of the cloud, but there was no wind to lift so much as a single floating hair.

Tamzin was saying, 'This is Lindsey, Jim. You'll see her a lot, I expect, this next fortnight. Isn't it rotten we've got to be at school and can't show her everything ourselves?'

'You got ter-morrer, Sunday.' He was twitching his overhanging eyebrows at Lindsey in the fierce way that passed, with him, for a smile.

'Church,' said Tamzin, 'for one thing.'

'And for another,' said Rissa, swinging the suitcase, 'the weather will be awful. Pity it can't last the way it was this morning.'

The ferryman shook his head, causing his little golden ear-rings to tremble, twinkling in the dark heavy air.

'No good couldn't come er that caper, gal. July in November, and late November too – tidn't nacheral, choose how. Stands to reason you gotter pay fer them frolics, see.'

Suddenly, his cloud of soft shining hair was lifted and flung aside, as if it might have been the blown froth upon a pail of warm new milk. The three girls glanced uneasily over their shoulders to the north-west, and Lindsey shivered at the icy touch of the wind that gusted past them. They could follow the track of the gust even after it had passed them, by the whipping away of Snowey Peplow's drooping cloud of blue-ish chimney-smoke, between the village and the sea; and by the anxious clustering of sheep that crowded on the saltings.

'Dang it,' remarked Jim Decks. 'Some hem queer business somewhere. Yew never know whur the next one's coming from. Howsumdever, I'll lay we gits the trouble when we gits that great old cloud. Comes low, don't she? An' she come agin the wind – so far as us knows whur the wind lays, that is. That look to me more like South Pacific weather, that do, nor what it do like Channel blow.'

'Are any of the smacks out, Jim?' Tamzin asked anxiously, looking up and down the river. She knew them all so well – had known them from earliest childhood – and especially the *Stormy Petrel* owned by old Jim's young Jim, Walter Goddard's *Samphire*, and Charlie Briggs's old *Meteor*.

'Larst one come in midday. That wur Hookey and them. Went straight insides the Conqueror, they did, and I'll lay they're drunk as lords be now. Never could hold his drink, couldn't Hookey.' Reaching inside the open doorway of his black wooden hut, he stowed the wool and sausages upon a shelf above the lintel. 'Reckon I better go and help our Jimmy batten down old *Stormy Petrel* fer the night. We got a dirty lotter weather brewin' up, or I ent never seen none. An' lucky we'll be iffen so we finds all us boats sitting whur us tied un, come the mornin'.'

He had turned his vast square shoulders and was padding softly towards the wooden jetty, his red rubber sea-boots making little noise except for a rustling in the dry shingle. Lindsey picked up the case she had been sitting on and Rissa swung hers across to the other hand.

'Tea,' said Tamzin, and they walked together up the

Hard, past the William the Conqueror Inn where the lamps were lit already, making primrose patches on the peeling weather-board frontage; past the offices of the Harbour Commissioners, empty for the week-end; past the tall white Harbour Mast with its dangling black storm cone, like a devil's ice-cream cornet hanging handy in the upper air; past the old Ship Inn Cottage and the corner of the grocer's garden, to the double wooden gates that stood open at the end of the short vicarage drive.

Lindsey was saying, 'I'm longing to see Diccon and the snails. And shall we see the ponies before morning? Oh, that must be the Martello tower, mustn't it? Where you lived last holidays. What fun it must have been! I wish I'd been here then.' They were walking down the drive now, past the high banked tamarisks on the one side and the winter-bare rose-pergola on the other. 'I can't think how you grow anything at all in all this shingle.'

'Oh, but they jolly well do!' said Rissa. 'Mrs Grey has very bright green fingers. You should see it in the summer.'

Then the front door in the porch burst open and a small boy in corduroys rushed out of it.

'Oh, there you are! I thought you were never coming. Isn't the sky simply super? Do you think we're going to have a blizzard? I say, I suppose you're Lindsey? We've been having an awful job finding a decent towel for you, after Mrs Briggs spilt the blackberry jelly in the washing-basket, but in the end we put one of father's – '

They were in the porch now, and Tamzin was thinking to herself that it would be just as well if they got safely past the umbrella stand without Diccon remembering that he had a grand haul of snails and

earwigs in the bottom of it, but this crisis was averted
by the appearance of Tamzin's mother in the kitchen
doorway as soon as they had stepped into the hall. Then
almost immediately, in the middle of the welcomes, the
Vicar of Westling walked out from his study, where he
had been making notes for the morrow's sermons and
no one could properly hear anyone else for all the
family talk there was in the hall.

There were the two cats, the grey and the ginger,
all among everyone's feet and being picked up and
passed around. There was Rissa saying what fun the
squall had been, and Tamzin saying how most peculiar
the sky was looking and how funny their ears had felt.
There was the Vicar saying he hadn't noticed anything
unusual and going to look at the glass; Mrs Grey saying
the boys had not arrived yet; Lindsey saying what a
perfect place she thought Westling was and Diccon
saying *please* wouldn't anyone come and see his per-
forming centipedes, of which he had seven in the
wood-shed.

In a momentary lull, Mrs Grey was heard to say that
tea would be ready in ten or fifteen minutes and, as it
was already nearly dark, what with the approaching
storm and the time of year, there began a rush into
the garden and round to the stable so that Lindsey
could see the two ponies while anything could be seen
at all without a lantern. They were both waiting by
the paddock gate; the white half-Arab, Cascade, that
was Tamzin's, and the small brown gipsy pony Banner,
who belonged to Diccon and had been rescued from a
life of drudgery and hunger, but was now as plump and
mischievous as any happy pony should be.

'We'll bring them in now for the night,' said Tamzin
with her hand on the gate. But even as she spoke the
stuffy air was split and shattered by a fresh squall from

the south, blowing them against the wooden rails like scraps of paper whisked against a grating.

'We did say, "Oh for a breath of air",' gasped Rissa, grinning round at Tamzin with her loose hair flung across her face.

'It's all right, ponies!' Tamzin was shouting into the screaming squall, but the ponies didn't hear her. They were rearing and pawing. Their manes and tails streamed from them and their ears lay flattened under blown-back forelocks.

A racketing rattle was a galvanized bucket coming bowling down the stable-yard, and a clank and clatter was the two dustbin-lids flying on to the pebbly back path.

'It'll go as quickly as it came,' yelled Lindsey hopefully, hanging on to the gatepost, and a door crashed to, with a noise like a gun, in the cottages just over the wall.

The ponies wheeled, bucked, snorted, and galloped away down the paddock. The silver-plane trees by the wall were leaning and bowing, waving like seaweed in a ground-swell. Tamzin, glancing up through little stinging wisps of her hair, saw that the dark cloud was now nearly overhead, having swollen so enormously as to blot out half the sky.

From the house Mrs Grey called anxiously, but no one could have heard her. Tamzin was having enough difficulty preventing her words from being blown clean away before they reached Rissa and Lindsey.

'I'm not so sure . . . that this one will . . . blow over as . . . soon as all that. We'd better . . . try to fetch the ponies.'

'May as well,' Rissa shouted back, 'in case it gets any . . . worse.'

Tamzin was struggling with the gate. It was firmly

clamped shut by the violence of the wind, and remained so until the combined power of all three of them hauled it half-way open, at which point it was immediately snatched from them and hurled the other way, coming to rest with a crash that shook the fence from end to end.

'At least it's open,' said Rissa breathlessly.

'Jolly good job we haven't got Diccon with us,' said Tamzin, leaning on the wind as if it were a solid wall.

'I think I'd be most useful,' Lindsey said at the top of her voice, 'if I stay here and see it doesn't shut again.'

Tamzin nodded, her plaits standing out strangely down the wild wind. She and Rissa bent themselves into it, like arctic explorers into a blizzard. They were pushing out across the paddock; past their feet flew wisps of whirling hay and straw from corners of the stable-yard and all around them madly danced the dead autumn leaves, flung about like golden-brown confetti.

It was like swimming; forging a way down the paddock with the high wind ramping straight across their path, pushing them sideways like the current in a river. There was the same deliberate effort to breathe, the same turning of the face sideways as from a rush of water, and the same slanting from one's proper direction in order to reach the right point in the end.

Lindsey was hanging over the back-flung gate, the fullness of her pleated skirt blown through the bars, like a dark sail straining to the wind. She watched the others moving down the paddock to where the ponies huddled in a corner under the lee of the wall, out of the full force of the wind's race. She noticed with relief that these ponies were not difficult to catch, the way Nanti sometimes was, at home in Surrey, and that Tamzin and Rissa already had the halters on them. They were coming out now into the storm's path, and the wind hit them broadside on. The ponies wouldn't face it. They reared again, pulling back, and their manes and tails were like smoke blowing madly from a bush-fire. The wind in Lindsey's eyelashes made it difficult for her to see, the wind in her ears made a singing and buzzing, and suddenly she was bitterly cold and shivering as she waited, watching.

Something was clanking down the village street. Perhaps a dustbin or the tin roof from a hen-coop. The sky was very dark. The purple fan-shaped cloud spread low and brooding overhead. In the paddock the ponies had pulled back into their corner, but Tamzin and Rissa were dragging off their jerseys, folding them across the ponies' eyes and tying the sleeves behind the flattened ears. That was a good idea: the sort of thing Tamzin would think of, but she, Lindsey, never. And now the ponies were coming, and perhaps . . . perhaps . . . yes, she was almost sure the wind was falling. There was going to be another lull and they would get the ponies in without more trouble, making fast the stable doors and windows against the worst that surely was to come.

And the wind dropped.

Suddenly, the wind had gone. But the air was so full of the troubled growl of the sea and of the singing in the ears that one felt as if the wind were still there, but somehow standing still and moaning to itself. Lindsey felt light-headed, watching the ponies approach towards the gate that she held open. She felt as one feels coming too swiftly out of a heavy dream, as if suspended between two places, being neither in this one nor that.

'It won't be for long this time,' Tamzin was saying

... their manes and tails were like smoke blowing madly

as she hurried through into the stable-yard, the white pony dancing at her side with nostrils wide and trembling.

'And when we get it next,' said Rissa, following with Banner, 'I'll bet you we've got it for the night. And won't I know it, biking back to Dunsford after tea!'

Lindsey shut the gate, shaking it to make sure it was secure. Then, slowly, she glanced up, suddenly aware, in the marrow of her bones, of the presence of her old fear. And even as she glanced the great cloud tore itself in two and flung a spear of lightning to the sea.

Then Lindsey's stomach turned to water as the fear took hold of her, and the sound of the thunder smothered every other sound, even to the singing in her own ears.

'I'm coming!' she said in answer to Tamzin's call, and made herself walk calmly.

CHAPTER 3

DEVIL'S STEW

*

BACK in the house, in the cheerfulness of the lamplit sitting-room, Lindsey heard Tamzin saying, 'This is Meryon. You know, the pirate's descendant. His ancestor was the famous Tonkin Fairbrass.' And there was a vague impression of an immensely powerful and very dark-haired boy of perhaps sixteen or so: but all she was really thinking about was the rising of the wind outside beyond the flowered curtains, and whether there would be another crash of thunder.

'Hallo,' she said gravely, smiling just a little. But she was thinking it would really be rather too much to hope for – one clap and no more at all, in a storm of this dimension.

'And Roger,' said Tamzin. 'He makes wireless sets and plays a violin and is sort of Rissa's cousin.'

And now the impression was of a younger boy, less vivid in colour and character but with a sensible, quiet serenity that Lindsey liked. And still it hadn't thundered again, and still the wind was rising, howling round the isolated house.

Rissa was excited by the weather, her cheeks flushed and eyes bright as she rushed between the kitchen and the sitting-room carrying tea-things with Diccon.

Tamzin was talking to Roger by the window. 'Mother said she didn't think you'd come when she saw the storm cone was up, but I didn't suppose weather would ever make much difference to you two.'

37

'I think we rather like weather,' said Roger.

'We brought torches,' Meryon said. 'It'll be dark as a tomb going back.'

'Rissa will be blown back,' Tamzin said, 'but you'll have to cut across the wind.'

Diccon said, passing them, 'There are hot potato cakes for tea, and chocolate cake.'

'Can I do anything?' Lindsey asked, but it seemed all was on the table except the teapot, and Mrs Grey was seeing to that herself.

'The thing that's rather worrying everyone about to-night,' Meryon was saying, 'is the very high tide. That, with this wind, and from the south as well.'

'Does the river ever overflow?' Lindsey asked, thinking to herself that even this would be as nothing, if only it wouldn't thunder any more. It wasn't that she was actually *afraid* of thunder. It was more a sort of power it had over her, as heights have over some people; a power of reducing one to uselessness.

'Well no, not seriously,' Meryon answered, placing chairs around the table. 'But the sea-wall isn't awfully good in patches. Last year it gave way in two weak spots and we had quite a bit of a flood around the castle.'

Tamzin said, 'And that was when we had high winds and high tides together, just like now.'

'Not really just like now,' said Roger. 'Listen to the wind. This really is something, this time.'

Lindsey listened, as she had been doing since they came in and Tamzin had drawn the coloured curtains: listened, as she went on doing all through tea, above the cheerful conversations and her own answers to friendly questions. She hoped that the calm, alert side of her, which sat and talked and smiled and ate with the others, was all that they saw of Lindsey Thornton, because the other side of her that listened abstractedly was one to be ashamed of. And still it didn't thunder.

But the wind, oh, the wind that rocked the house and shook the windows . . .

'What time d'you make it?' Meryon was saying to Rissa, looking at his watch and accepting a scone at the same time.

'Nearly six. No, I'll have bread-and-butter, I think. But my watch has been all over the place to-day. I forgot to wind it.'

The Vicar opened his gold Hunter. 'I make it a quarter to.'

'Well, judging by that clock,' said Mrs Grey, looking to the mantelpiece, 'which says five past, it must be just about ten to.'

Rissa threw back her Egyptian hair and guffawed nearly as loudly as the wind.

'It does make us sound a crazy party!' Tamzin grinned, pushing the scones towards Roger.

Roger said, 'But crazy people are far nicer than ordinary ones. No thank you, but I'll have another sandwich, please.'

'What really worries me,' Mrs Grey said, 'is the thought of you people who have to get back across the Marsh to-night.'

'We've got waterproofs,' Roger said.

'And torches,' said Meryon.

'And we don't mind about the weather,' said Rissa.

'I dare say,' said Mrs Grey, 'but I still don't like it very much. What time is high water, does anyone know?'

'Must be around midnight,' said Tamzin. 'It was at midday when we went up the river.'

'Twelve-ten,' Meryon said. He was helping Diccon

to pour himself some more milk. 'Plenty of time. But all the same I think we ought to be starting pretty soon. We shan't have the wind against us, of course, but it won't be exactly behind us, so we may have rather a push.'

'I think you're wise,' said the Vicar. 'There'll probably be heavy rain later, and it'll drive in down your neck with this wind. Far better to get home while it's dry.'

Tamzin pushed back her chair and went across to the window, parting the curtains.

'But it isn't,' she said. 'It isn't dry; it's raining already. Look at it running down the glass.'

'Couldn't hear it for the noise the wind's making,' Roger said. 'Oh well, I suppose we'd still better get going, before it gets worse.'

Mrs Grey got up and looked through the window herself.

'Oh dear,' she said. 'Perhaps we oughtn't to have let you come. It really does look dreadful. Richard, I don't see how we can let them go out in all this. They have to walk more than two miles; quite a bit more, with Meryon and Roger.'

Her husband was carefully tipping out the last shreds of tobacco from his pouch.

'Well need they, my dear? Unless of course the telephone is already out of order. I should say most of the lines on the Marsh will be down before morning.'

Tamzin whipped round from the window.

'You mean they can all stay the night? Oh, what a stunning notion, Mother! Shall I go and see if the phone is all right?'

'Your father's notion, really,' said Mrs Grey uncertainly. 'I don't know what on earth we could do about beds. Though the more one looks at the weather the more one sees how hopeless it would be even to keep one's feet, in it.'

'As if beds mattered!' said Tamzin. 'We never slept in them in camp, or in the tower. I'll go and try the phone.'

'If anybody's not sleeping in their beds,' said Diccon suddenly over the top of his stripy beaker, 'I want to be one of them.'

Meryon said, calling after Tamzin, 'Hold hard a minute, Tamzin! Fix up anything you like for Rissa, but Jiminy, Roger and I've never been kept in by a gale and we aren't starting now.'

Rissa looked at him furiously.

'Meryon – '

But everyone else was talking at once now, and the gale as loudly as anyone. The house moaned and groaned, creaked and rattled and shivered, and Tamzin went into the hall and picked up the telephone.

Mrs Grey was saying, 'If, as Tamzin says, no one really cares either way about beds, there seems to be no reason left at all why anyone should get themselves soaked. Now let me see; there's Lindsey in the small spare room – '

'But I'm used to sleeping rough, too,' said Lindsey.

' – which leaves us the second spare bed and the camp bed for the other three.'

'There is the sofa, of course,' suggested the Vicar.

'So there is. A bit short and narrow, perhaps, and we shall have to use coats for extra blankets.'

'She's got through,' said Diccon, looking in at the doorway.

'Oh good! Thank you, Roger; all the cakes and things go out into the kitchen, but put them in the tins, won't you? Because the cats would commit any crime for cake. The plates and cups in the scullery,

Lindsey dear. Now what was I saying? No, Diccon, you can't possibly sleep in the bath. Now do let me think ... Rissa in the camp bed in Tamzin's room. Roger on the sofa and Meryon in the other spare room because he's taller. Don't go away, Dicky! It's almost bedtime already.'

Suddenly Lindsey found she had forgotten about the thunder and was being swept up in the stream of this surprising day, in which nothing seemed to happen according to plan and even the storm outside was mightier and queerer by far than the ordinary one: but all these people here in the vicarage took everything with a matter-of-fact calmness that Lindsey found infectious. All of them, that was, except Diccon, who was at that moment face downwards on the carpet under the table in such an uproar of rage and grief that the roar of the gale was almost eclipsed.

'It can't be helped, old man,' his mother was saying. 'We had tea later than usual and so bedtime just seems a bit earlier.'

'But it isn't *fair*!' wailed Diccon passionately. 'I didn't *know* tea was later, and I haven't shown Lindsey my centipedes or fed my snails or *any*thing.'

Lindsey stopped in the doorway with her pile of plates and saucers.

'Perhaps if he showed them to me quickly?'

'We-ell – ' said Mrs Grey, feeling her authority slipping. But Diccon was already up and out of the room. She could just hear him saying, 'I've got five – sniff – under the stairs, because they always – sniff – escape from the umbrella stand.'

Then there was the washing-up of tea-things, followed, for Lindsey, by unpacking in a bedroom so exposed to wind and weather that it was almost like a crow's-nest, and hunting round with Tamzin for spare sheets and blankets for the camp bed ('We can lend them some pyjamas, but what on earth can we do about tooth-brushes?'), then the wild excitement of being drawn into a game of 'Murder' at Meryon's suggestion, and playing it in the thick darkness of the gale-rocked attics, where you didn't know whether you were more scared of the cold hands creeping round your neck or of the storm that screamed among the chimneys and shook the floor beneath your tiptoeing feet.

And there was the weird interlude when Meryon was the corpse, sending up his blood-curdling screech into the storm and being found by Rissa, the detective, with her torch. He was lying huddled at the top of the stairs, his wild black hair across his forehead and his arms flung out realistically. The questioning, by lamp-light in Tamzin's high bedroom, produced no clues at all, and almost Lindsey began to imagine there must have been some other, unknown player. It didn't do to be seen looking over your shoulder, away into the shadow-hung corners, but it certainly was very peculiar.

'And where were you at the time of the murder?' Rissa was questioning Lindsey, the last of the witnesses.

'On the attic stairs.'

'Did anyone pass you, just before?'

'Oh no. I'd have been sure to feel or hear anyone, the stairs are so narrow.'

'Did you hear any movement on the attic landing?'

'Only the corpse's scream. Oh, I think someone giggled, somewhere.'

'They did,' said Meryon, grinning. 'It sounded like Tamzin.'

'The corpse,' said Rissa crushingly, 'isn't allowed to speak.'

43

Meryon bowed, his shadow dipping over the wall.

'Someone *must* be boggling their evidence,' Rissa said finally. 'And only the murderer is allowed to tell lies. No one passed Lindsey on the stairs, no one passed Tamzin in the west attic and Roger saw no one in Tamzin's doorway. Then who murdered Meryon at the top of the stairs? I say it must have been Roger. No one else could have done it without someone hearing them. You, Roger?'

'No,' said Roger. 'Not me.'

'The wind's so screaming loud,' said Tamzin. 'Perhaps we just didn't hear whoever it was – any of us.'

'Was it you?' guessed Rissa.

'No.'

'Well, there isn't anybody else who *could*. Stop grinning, Meryon; you're dead.'

'Perhaps it was an Unknown Player,' hazarded Lindsey uneasily.

'It wasn't you?' Rissa plumped.

'Oh, no!'

'But it must have been *one* of you! Someone must have done it.'

'Well, it wasn't me,' said Tamzin, Roger, and Lindsey all together.

'Ask the corpse,' said Tamzin, almost glancing quickly behind her, but not quite. 'There's the supper gong.'

'Come on, Meryon! Who dunnit?' asked Rissa.

Meryon bowed again, mockingly.

'Well?' said Rissa.

'By my own hand,' said Meryon.

'Oh, I say! Suicide isn't allowed, is it? Is suicide allowed, Rissa?' Roger objected.

But Rissa was already racing down to supper.

It was while they were washing up the supper things that the banging was heard on the door.

'Listen!' said Tamzin. 'Isn't that someone at the door?'

Everyone stopped talking and looked at everyone else for a moment, cups, knives, and dish-mop held suspended.

'It's only the wind, I expect,' Rissa said. 'Everything's rattling and banging.'

'It was the door,' insisted Tamzin. 'I'll go and see.'

She dropped the dish-mop with a slither into the soapy water and went through the scullery and penthouse, drying her hands as she went. The back door was snatched immediately from her grasp, crashing against the wall and letting in a wind like demons. Two more doors inside the house banged loudly and Jim Decks the ferryman walked in, gripped the back door and forced it shut again. He looked at Tamzin under his sou'wester through a blown wet thicket of beard and hair and whiskers. Down from his shining oilskins the water ran in pools upon the floor.

'Three hours to high water,' he said, 'and the river's overflowin' already. It's this wind what's piled 'er up, see.'

'Oh, Jim!'

'It'll be a snorter,' Rissa said, standing in the scullery doorway with a tea-towel in her hands.

'Yew never spoke a truer word, gal. I ent seen weather like this lot, not since I were a tiddler. Reg'lar devil's stew boiling up.' He peered at Tamzin again, the rain-drops running from his nose and chin. 'Yer pa anywheres around?'

'I'll see if I can fetch him, Jim. He was swotting at his sermons. Saturday night, you know.'

The old man shrugged massively and fresh showers sprinkled on the doormat.

'I doubt he'll have time fer no sermonizing, come the morning. Seems to me we'll want all hands on deck, so to speak, iffen this lot blow up the way she shapes to, and the glass still falling fit to knock the bottom outer the barometer. There's some as'll be flooded out, we reckon. Me and Wally Goddard and them, back in the Conqueror, we thought the Vicar might open up the Mission Hall fer 'em, see, jus' in case.'

Tamzin was hooking her towel on the scullery door. 'I'll go and tell him now.'

Meryon looked at his watch.

'Is it really going to be as bad as that, Jim?'

'We-ell – I reckon so. We already got old Snowey Peplow out. Him what got that liddle house down river. Wally and our Jimmy and me, we bin and took Jimmy's punt and fetched him a half-hour back, when we saw the way she wur blowing up; him and all his stuff what'd fit insides the boat, see. We-ell, reckon we can fit ole Snowey in at our place easy enough, but, as we see it, looks like next it'll be Shirty Smeed and them, out behind the church. I'll lay they got water round three sides now, so low-lyin' as they be. An' then if the sea-wall busts – 'Evenin', Vicar!'

'Good evening, Jim! Come along inside! I have a fire in the study.'

'Thankin' yew, Vicar, but I won't come in, so tedious wet as I am. I come to say as we just got Snowey Peplow out. River wuz lapping on his door-step and near three hours to high water. I'll lay we're fer it to-night, sir.'

'I was afraid so, Jim; I was afraid so, myself. There's too much wind altogether.'

'Ar, that there be, sir; fer a tide as high as this'n. It's the sea-wall what we're worriting over. Don't see how 'er'll stand it. Then there's them Smeeds, out back er the church. They'll cop it, sir.'

The Vicar nodded thoughtfully, gazing profoundly at nothing in particular.

Old Jim went on, 'Wally an' me an' them, we reckon we might have flooding right in the village, Vicar. Especial in them low-lyin' lots along the river and back er the sea-wall. We ent seen nothing like this weather, none of us, only when we was ocean-going and layin' in hurricane latitudes.'

'The Mission Hall stands higher than most in the village,' said the Vicar.

'Yessir. We thought of that, sir.'

'And the Sailors' Institute, and of course the vicarage.'

'Yessir.'

'Perhaps I'd better get my macintosh and look things over, Jim. We may need temporary beds . . . '

Tamzin said, 'There are all those blankets in the Sailors' Institute. The ones for shipwrecked sailors. Oh, Daddy, can't we come too? All the five of us? We could help no end if you would let us.'

Rissa said, 'You'll want lots of hot cups of tea if you're really having rescued families. We could make them in relays on a primus.'

'You might want help with the rescue work,' Meryon suggested.

'And it doesn't matter a bit what time we go to bed,' said Roger, 'because it isn't school in the morning.'

Lindsey said, 'It would be quite all right about me. I mean, Mother wouldn't mind, and I could tie a scarf over my ears.'

Old Jim carefully avoided looking at them in case

47

they should be trying to get him on their side, for you never knew what set-up that Tamzin would be brewing. But the Vicar blinked at them doubtfully, wondering where his wife was.

'We-ell ...'

'Oh, *good*!' said Tamzin, very loudly, because you had to shout to hear yourself above the gale. 'We'll be ready in less than two shakes.'

They had all vanished, all five of them, in a twinkling of an eye. The Vicar shook his head and smiled at Jim, and the old man wrinkled up his leathery face in reply.

'I know, sir! I've 'ad dealings with 'em, meself.'

CHAPTER 4

AGAINST THE GALE

*

TAMZIN and Lindsey stepped out from the back door that was held open by Jim and the Vicar, and were immediately blown down flat upon their faces.

'Are you all right?' Tamzin yelled, lifting herself carefully to her hands and knees, and Lindsey's answering shout, from only a yard or two away, was like a voice heard on a summer's evening across the breadth of a valley, reassuring Tamzin, who was remembering the measles and the ears.

'All right!'

The gale raced past them and over them with the strength and frenzy of madness. It was as if all the world's atmosphere were rushing furiously by; and far above was heard the long unearthly shriek that sometimes travels with a hurricane.

'You . . . have to . . . lean into . . . it,' roared Meryon, hunching his way up the path, the shape of him scarcely visible in the blindness of a night lit only by a few remote stars.

'Goldeye's chimbley's gorn,' Jim shouted, and Tamzin, looking up into rain that fell like a waterfall, saw upon the grocer's roof the unfamiliar shape of a broken chimney, stark against the ragged storm-clouds.

Turning into the village street they had the gale behind them and everyone at once leaned back at an acute angle, their coats wildly flapping round bent knees. It was difficult not to start running, hurtling up the village too fast for legs to keep up.

'You can sit down ... on it!' Roger grinned. 'Just ... like a chair.'

Something came banging, crashing, leaping up the street behind them, and they forged to the roadside, hastening to avoid injury by unseen missiles of the storm.

The gale raced past them and over them with the strength and frenzy of madness

'Some pore codger's fowl-'ouse,' Jim observed. He was almost certainly shouting to the full capacity of his very powerful lungs, but in the ears of the others the voice was as one heard on coming slowly out of an anaesthetic, dim and infinitely far away.

They began to allow themselves to be blustered up the street again. It was easy to see where they were going because of the occasional lighted cottage window, close beside the street. One of these had plants in pots upon the sill inside, boldly silhouetted against the lamp light of the room. Through one or two a family could be seen beyond the rain-washed glass, their chairs drawn up around the fire; but mostly the cottages were sunk in the darkness of the night, for the kitchen was almost always the heart of the home in country such as this was, and the kitchens lay towards the back.

Now and again, as they leaned back against the storm's thrust, old Jim would make some bellowed observation which might be heard by some of the party and certainly would not be heard by others:

'That's old Wally's apple-tree gorn finished.'

'See that, Vicar? I'll lay that's half the tiles orf of Mus. Budden's.'

'Now whur in thunder'd that old branch come from? Mind you don' lay yerselves out over she.'

They reached the Sailors' Institute and Mr Grey hauled himself up to the gate, hand-over-hand along the railings, then staggered up the short open path to the door as one not entirely sober. The others struggled after him, rain streaming down their faces and already running into wellingtons. They were looking at the row of lit-up windows in the billiard-room as if they were beholding some miracle of peace and stillness in a world of noise and chaos. There were even men playing billiards, just as if outside the world were not a howling desolation, with people's apple-trees and chimney-pots thrown down, and even their homes in hourly danger.

The Vicar turned the handle, the door blew open inwards with a loud, dull crash and all the hanging lamps above the billiard-table dipped their lights in the inrush of the wind. Everyone crowded inside and two young fishermen fought the door back into its place, touched their foreheads to the Vicar and returned to their game. Suddenly there was the most amazing sense of peace. Lindsey had a queer sensation that she was rocking slightly on her feet, as one might still feel the sensation of pedalling after long and arduous bicycling. Outside the wind shrieked and roared around the building, but inside was the comfortable click of billiard-balls and the thick dark fog of plug tobacco smoke.

'Dirty weather, Vicar,' said Albert Clench, the Institute caretaker. 'I dessay you come about them blankets?' He was a very heavy man, too heavy and too old for fishing now, but nicely suited with his present job of caretaking.

The Vicar was absently watching the play. To-night there were no other spectators, for most of Westling's men were with their boats in the Harbour, anxiously working to make them safe against the gale.

'Very dirty, Albert,' he agreed. 'Yes, that's what we came about, though I'm hoping we shan't need to use them.'

'The wife she got 'em all out a while ago, sir, and set 'em round the stove. We thought you'd likely fare to want 'em.'

'Oh, thank you, Albert. I see young Smeed isn't here. Have you any news of how they're weathering this?'

Old Albert shook his head gravely.

'Pretty bad, sir, we reckon. He wur here a half-hour back, but his old dad looked in and fetched him out, see; said they got the water in the gardin and fare to want 'is help.'

'Stands to reason,' said the ferryman, 'the crazy place they put their liddle bungalow.'

'I told 'em, sir, as I reckoned you'd welcome 'em in

here, 'iffen so there's danger to the 'ouse,' finished Albert.

'Yes, of course, Albert. I think perhaps we should make ready what we can, in case we have more guests than we expect. These five youngsters here have come to lend a hand. I know Mrs Clench can't keep the upper rooms in daily order, but if she will provide the brooms and dusters my working gang will soon have everything ship-shape.'

'Yessir. I'll get 'em now, sir, and light the lamps up there. And p'raps you'd like to come and look-see at them blankets?'

Waterproofs and wellingtons were being pulled off and hung or propped to drip around the stove.

'My stockings are wet as dish-cloths,' Rissa said, peeling them off. 'I'll have to go bare-legged until they're dry. Roger, get me my sandals from my raincoat pocket, please; you're nearest the stove.'

Roger was drying his face on his handkerchief. He dug down into the pockets, sending fresh drops splashing on the floor.

'Catch!'

Jim Decks looked with fatherly disapproval at the dangling drying stockings.

'Stands to reason they're wet. They ent no good fer the job. You want proper stout oiled wool, same as we have. Now that'll hold the water like a sponge.'

'Yes, I know, Jim. But it was a peaceful summer's day when I left home this morning. These aren't even my wellingtons.' She was buckling on her sandals.

'Anyone what had a barometer'd have seen it weren't true fair weather,' Jim persisted. 'Lowest reading as I ever saw in my life, these parts. Stands to reason –'

'It wasn't only her,' said Tamzin, spreading out her

raincoat. 'I thought so too. We didn't look at the glass. Did you, Meryon?'

Meryon was wringing out his trousers at the knees.

'I saw it was too low for any sense, but I just supposed the thing had gone bust.'

'We haven't a barometer,' said Lindsey. 'And I was in the train. I thought the weather looked wonderful,' she admitted.

'What did the forecast say? Anyone hear it?' asked Roger.

'Of course,' said old Jim. 'Said charnce of gales, but ter-day's outlook unsettled. Howsumdever, no one round here don't fare to take much notice of that announcer what they've took to having lately. He don't 'cast the weather like that old 'un did, 's fact.'

'Oh, Jim,' said Rissa. 'They only read what they're given. It's just the same with all of them.'

The ferryman waggled his head, his little ear-rings bobbing.

'Donchew believe it, gal. Stands to reason –'

The house door opened and the Vicar came back into the billiard-room.

'Mrs Clench has left brooms and dusters at the foot of the stairs, and the lamps are lit ready. Tamzin, you know where the Institute crockery is kept – in the cupboard in the hall. We'd better have most of that out, and the primus and the tea and sugar. And the blankets in Mrs Clench's kitchen must go upstairs. Carry on as best you can, and ask Mrs Clench if you want to know anything. Jim and I are going to the Mission Hall, and then to see the water-level. You needn't wait, any of you, when you've done all you can. Far better to go home and get to bed.'

'All right, Dad! Don't worry; we'll be all right.'

There was the same struggle with the door again, the

same wild gust that sank the lamp-flames, the same abandoned crash behind the departing men. Then almost at once the whole performance over again as the two young fishermen, having finished their game, slammed out into the shrieking of the storm.

Tamzin and Lindsey had gathered up the working tools and were going up the narrow uncarpeted stairs with them. Rissa and Roger and Meryon were sorting crockery and stores on to the billiard-table and Roger was saying, 'I can only find two packets of tea. How many cups will that make, Rissa? Blowed if I remember if it's six teaspoonfuls or six ounces to a pot.'

'It isn't either,' Rissa said, 'unless you're five in family and like it pretty thick. If so, the usual recipe is a teaspoonful for each person and one for the pot.'

'Darned silly notion,' said Roger cheerfully. 'It can't matter to the pot.' He was groping in the shadows of the cupboard.

'It's just a saying,' Rissa said. 'And in any case it's much too strong that way. You can't taste the milk.'

Meryon put down a pile of saucers on the green baize of the table.

'No fisherman thinks tea is any good unless it'll float the spoon. Remember that, and if you're making it for any of them to-night you'd much better tip the whole packet in. I shouldn't think a little earth'd do it any harm, either, if you're running short.'

'Here's the sugar, lots of it,' said Rissa, peering into a large blue packet. 'Oh, there's a fly in it.'

'Hibernating for the winter, I expect,' said Roger. 'Nobody'll know if you don't say anything.'

Rissa fished it out with a teaspoon and dropped it in the stove.

'It was dead anyway. Now what do we do about milk? We can't –'

Suddenly there was the most tremendous bang.

Everyone stopped and stared at everyone else.

'Chimney,' said Roger, after a moment.

'It wasn't,' said Rissa. 'I've heard that bang before.'

'It was the lifeboat maroon,' Meryon said. 'Christopher! And on a night like this.'

The inner door flew open and Tamzin and Lindsey rushed in.

'Did you hear that? Lifeboat.'

'What a night for it!' said Lindsey, staring at the black rain-shiny windows. 'Though it hasn't thundered any more. Where is the lifeboat house? Nearby?'

'Gosh, no!' said Roger. 'Miles away.'

'Less than two,' corrected Meryon.

'Across the grazings and the beach,' finished Roger.

'They'll never get there!' Tamzin said anxiously. She stood on one of a row of chairs against the wall, her face pressed to the darkness of a window.

'Of course they will. They always have,' said Rissa briskly. 'I'm putting the tea and sugar in the crockery box, Meryon.'

'I don't see how they can launch her, or how she'll ever sail in this, let alone find any other vessel.' Tamzin was rubbing the window with her sleeve, but outside the darkness was impenetrable. 'It's simply crazy, crazy weather; roaring and ramping up the village.'

'She's supposed to be uncapsizable, this one,' Meryon said. 'So once they do launch her they ought to be all right. I'll take that crockery to the kitchen; I dare say you've got it sorted by now? And then I'm going out to see what's happening.'

'Two torches coming down the street already,' Tamzin said. 'You'd think they were always expecting it, the way they get out and away so quickly after the maroon.'

'I dare say they are, this weather,' Roger said. He was thrusting a hand inside his wellingtons. 'Pretty damp. Can't be helped, and I expect they'll be much damper before they're any drier.'

'You're not going, too?' Rissa exclaimed. 'And leaving us to cope with the refugees while you and Meryon have all the excitement?'

Roger hesitated, wellingtons in hand.

'I don't see that five of us can be needed to make cups of tea and share out blankets. Two, at the very most, I'd say; or one if it's only the Smeeds and Snowey Peplow; and we don't even know we're getting them.'

'Then we ought to draw lots, and in any case we've got to ask permission,' Tamzin said, jumping down from her chair.

Lindsey was picking spilt tea-leaves from the immaculate surface of the billiard-table. She said, 'We don't know that we could walk against it. It may have got worse since we came in, and before that Tamzin and I were blown clean over in the vicarage path.' She threw the tea-leaves on to the ashes under the stove.

Meryon came in again. 'I've turned the lamps low, upstairs. The gale's twice as loud up there as it is here. Anyone else coming along to ask about going to the lifeboat house? We'll have to hurry.' He was already pushing his feet down into wellingtons resistant with the damp, and at the same time lifting his oilskin raincoat off the peg above the stove.

'We ought to draw lots,' Tamzin repeated. 'No one wants to stay here who can go out and see them launch the boat.'

'I don't see why not,' Meryon said, heaving his coat on to his shoulders. 'There might be enough excitement for anyone here, if the sea-wall really goes.'

'All right,' Rissa said. 'You can stay then.'

Meryon turned an expressive bright blue glance on her. 'I didn't *want* to have to point out that this is one of those occasions when mere physical strength is what matters. But now you've made me. You three can be tremendously useful here if the worst happens, but what on earth use would you be, blown half across the Marsh?'

Lindsey said, a little diffidently because she was a visitor, 'That does seem sensible to me. I mean, I suppose we would be more useful than Meryon and Roger staying here, especially if they bring whole families in. And we wouldn't be half so valuable as they would, helping to haul the lifeboat out, or fighting through a wind like this one.'

'I'm pretty well as strong and hefty as Roger is,' Rissa said argumentatively. But Meryon said they were wasting valuable time, and that whoever was going would have to start at once if they were to get to the lifeboat house in time to be any use at all, especially as they had to call in at the vicarage for permission.

Roger said, 'Well, I'm ready, for one.' He was tying the strings of his sou'wester.

Tamzin suddenly swung round, talking quickly. 'Look: Lindsey and I'll stay here and Rissa go with you. I've thought it all out. She is the biggest of the three of us, and really Lindsey oughtn't to go (and I know Mother would say so) as she doesn't know the Marsh so well as we do, and the wind would be awfully bad for her ears.'

'I don't know the Marsh at all,' Lindsey said truthfully. 'Though I hope I shall, one day.'

'– and I'm staying partly because I'm the smallest and partly because Lindsey's my visitor,' finished Tamzin in a rush. 'Get your things on, Rissa, you donkey, and jolly well rush or you'll never be in time. If you

58

don't come straight back,' she added, as Rissa hauled her rubber boots on, 'we'll know you've got permission.'

Rissa, saying that it wasn't her idea and that they might just as well have drawn lots, flailed herself into her raincoat and jammed on her sou'wester, walking towards the door as she did so. Meryon turned the knob and everyone hung on with all their strength to stop the door crashing back against the wall, then all struggled as with an enemy to get it shut again behind the boys and Rissa.

Tamzin turned, panting, with her back against the door and her hands spread out upon it as if half expecting it to burst madly open again. 'You know,' she said, 'I really think it's worse. Did you hear that?'

Lindsey nodded. 'Sounded like another chimney somewhere. Are there any chimneys over this place?'

'Oh, I don't remember. I suppose there must be, but this is a newer building than most around here. Probably better built as well. It's the cottages that'll get the worst of it.'

They went into the billiard-room again.

'Better finish that job upstairs,' Tamzin said.

CHAPTER 5

HOT TEA AND BLANKETS

*

THEY had finished the sweeping and dusting in the two upper rooms. Lindsey had pushed a private misery off her chest in charging Tamzin with having sacrificed herself for her sake, because she was quite horribly certain that Tamzin would much rather have gone with the others to the lifeboat house. But Tamzin had replied, What rot, she naturally wanted to enjoy her own visitor's company, didn't she? And she wouldn't have missed the chance of helping with the rescued for any bribe on earth.

So Lindsey had felt a little less guiltily wretched, but not entirely so, and now they were occupied with carrying up more aired blankets from Mrs Clench's kitchen. Mrs Clench herself was fussing round them rather anxiously, her thin hands clasping and unclasping, her short-sighted eyes lifting frequently to the clock upon the mantelpiece as she watched a pan of cocoa come to the boil upon the range.

'Nearly ten o'clock, now, so it is, and you generally in bed afore nine, I know,' she said to Tamzin, who was folding the pile of rough brown blankets for easier carrying. 'Now see here, my maid, what I say is, you have a nice hot cup of cocoa when you done them blankets, and then Father'll see you safe home – won't you, Bert? Me and him might jus' as well bide up in case of need, fer I know I'll never shut me eyes till this lot blow over, what with the lifeboat out an' all.'

Albert Clench opened one eye and nodded vigorously.

He was dozing a little sheepishly in his windsor chair, his grey-stockinged feet stuck out upon the shiny brass fender, his grizzled chin bobbing gently on his vast navy chest.

Tamzin placed the last blanket squarely on her pile.

'It's very kind of you,' she said, in the tone of one who is about to refuse the kindness, 'but – well – I say, Lindsey, are you feeling tired?'

'Me? Gosh, no! Not with all this going on. I'm like Mrs Clench; I couldn't possibly sleep a wink until the storm blows over, or at least till the others come back from the lifeboat house and the tide has turned.'

Tamzin said, 'Then I think we'd rather stay, Mrs Clench, thank you very much. I expect Father'll come and fetch us if he and Mother really think we ought to go back.'

'Well now, I'm sure I don't know what to say. My head's all in a muddle with this wind a-racketing round the house fit to lift it off of its foundationses.' She was dodging between the glowing range and the table with the saucepan in her hand, trying dimly to see if she was treading on the incredibly old white cat whom she had adopted from a shipwreck long ago.

'It's all right, I've got her, mate,' said Albert, coming-to again at the welcome noises of supper. 'She's layin' round behind me somewheres.'

'She must be fowerteen be now, even if she wur only a young un when we 'ad 'er orf of the shipwreck,' said Mrs Clench in her rather plaintive voice as she poured out cups of foaming cocoa, the hot steam wisping up and misting over her glasses, making her more dim-sighted even than usual. She took them off and wiped them with her apron. 'I wouldn't like to step on 'er now, arter all them years and all what the pore thing's lived through. Now put them blankets down a minute and drink yer cocoa hot. There's biscuits in the tin here. Ee, but I don't rightly know what to do about the both of you, and me with me head that muddled. What do you say, Bert?' She raised her voice a little to overcome the combined noises of the gale outside and Albert drinking his cocoa inside. 'What'll us do about Miss Tamzin and her visitor?'

Albert sucked in another mouthful in the manner which some people imagine cools the cocoa, put down his cup upon the fender, wiped his mouth with the back of a hand like a doormat, then said with profound deliberation, as one who has given the matter a great deal of thought, 'Eh?'

'Parson's child,' shrilled Mrs Clench. 'What'll us do about un?'

Albert wiggled his stockinged toes in the warmth of the fire.

'Leave un be,' he said, to Tamzin's and Lindsey's great relief, then he reached a biscuit from the tin and leaned his ponderous bulk forward to dunk it in his cocoa.

Tamzin was just opening her mouth to say could they leave their cocoa to cool for five minutes while they took the rest of the blankets upstairs, when a crash in the region of the billiard-room caused everyone to turn and look, but naturally without being able to see anything more than Mrs Clench's lamp-lit kitchen, its closed door hung with a dark red plush curtain which billowed cheerfully in the draught.

'Door,' said Albert, poking his feet into his boots. 'That'll be yer pa, Tamzin, I'll lay.'

Albert was quite right, and a moment later the Vicar walked into the kitchen, still wearing his drenched waterproofs but in his stockinged feet because he had left his wellingtons in the porch. Albert rose stiffly to his feet and Lindsey and Tamzin dumped their blankets back upon the table.

'Hallo, Dad! We've finished except for taking up these blankets. Did the others go out to the lifeboat house?'

Her father was dabbing his face. 'They did, they did. Very foolish, but so many others were going from the village, and they went in charge of Jim. He isn't in the crew any more now, you know; a man has to give up some day. Now, Tamzin and Lindsey; I've got some work for you if you still feel like tackling it, but if you're at all tired bed's the place.'

Mrs Clench nodded earnestly. 'That's what I just bin saying, Vicar, only they would have it they wasn't.'

'We really aren't,' Tamzin said.

'I shouldn't think anyone could be,' said Lindsey.

'Oh well, in that case I'll leave my refugees in your hands. I rather want to see how the houses round the Point are faring, as they're so close to the river. So the job for you now is hot tea and blankets for the Smeeds, the Upjohns and Snowey Peplow. They're drying themselves as best they can round the billiard-room stove, except for three of their menfolk who'll be looking in later. Come along and do the best you can for them.'

Mrs Clench called after them as they turned to go through the door. 'I'll 'ave me big kettle on in a jiffy. Save you fiddling with that old primus fer this lot, anyways. And shall Father look out them camp beds, sir? You won't want to bed down the women on the boards, so long as there's beds to share round, and you might have children here next, God forbid!'

The Vicar stood inclining his head to pick out Mrs Clench's shrill voice from the shriller voice of the storm. Then he nodded, the wet grey ends of his hair flopping limply on his temples. 'Thank you; yes, that would be most useful. A pity we haven't more of both blankets and beds – I rather fear we're going to need them – but they were of course only intended for a few ship-wrecked sailors.'

'Ar,' said Albert solemnly, rocking back slightly on his feet to balance the rounded heaviness of his front. 'I'll lay no one in this village reckoned then as one day us'd be rescuing ourselves. I'll range them camp beds up in the further upstairs room, sir, shall I?'

'Thank you, Albert.'

In the billiard-room Tamzin and Lindsey were very soon left alone with the first refugees.

'Oh, Mrs Smeed, I am so sorry! What happened about all your furniture and things? And the fowls and sheep and everything? Is the water right up to the house?'

'Near enough, it was,' said Mrs Smeed, in the slow courageous manner of Marsh women born to accept perils of sea and storm with quiet hearts and bulldog spirits. 'We saved a few bits of things, what Father and Bob's stowed away over in the Mission Hall. Being a bungalow we naturally didn't have no upstairs to stow things in. Father and Bob's over there now a-settling of the fowls what they fetched along in boxes.'

Snowey Peplow was rolling himself a cigarette with his own black tobacco.

'What he wanted were a tidy great spell what'd magic them pore sheep smaller so's he coulda boxed them too. He says to me, all us could do fer the pore wretches, he says, wuz to open up their gates and drive 'em roadwards. Gev 'em a sporting chance, he says to me, but I'll lay I don't smack eyes on 'em no more, he says, unless it's drownded.' Snowey's reedy voice was like a penny whistle, or a go-cart needing oil. He was very old, very solitary and a life-long bachelor but sociable withal. 'Wish I wuz a hem sight younger, and being useful with the lifeboat,' he said wistfully. 'I hully don't like 'em going out wi'out me, and me in the crew these forty year.'

'No good worriting,' said Mrs Upjohn placidly, though her kitchen was six inches deep in water. 'What will be, will be, and the Lord will provide.' Drawing nearer to the stove, she clasped her hands across her stomach and smiled at Tamzin and Lindsey.

'We've got some tea nearly ready for you, anyway,' said Tamzin. 'I know that's not much, but it's something.' Her eye discovered the almost empty coal-bucket. 'We'd better tip this lot on the stove and ask Mrs Clench about some more, with all these clothes and things to dry.'

For nearly an hour Tamzin and Lindsey worked about the Sailors' Institute. They strung up washing-lines borrowed from Mrs Clench, in zigzags under the ceiling between the hanging oil-lamps, and helped to drape wet possessions over them to dry in the stoked-up heat from the little stove. They made relays of strong tea for husbands and fathers who came in from time to time with further rescued oddments from the cottages and gardens, and when the lowered paraffin in the oil-lamps began to cause the lights to weaken, they turned them out and filled them, one by one, from Albert Clench's Institute store, which Mrs Clench had to find for them as Albert had long since gone to join the Vicar's rescue party.

The wild evening was advancing towards midnight when the door flew open with a roar like lions charging, and in crowded all the abundant Lillycrop family; father, mother, and their ten astonishingly named children, of whom Tamzin could at first only recognize Hydrangea, Minerva, and Ur because all the others were practically extinguished beneath mountains of blankets and mats and precious ornaments and other salvage from their cottage.

'What a blessing they've brought blankets,' Lindsey said to Tamzin as the Lillycrops hurled themselves in mass-attack upon the door to shut it. 'We'd never have had enough otherwise.'

Snowey was drawing out more chairs from the wall to set around the fireplace, and Mrs Upjohn and Mrs Smeed were edging their own chairs sideways to make more room.

'I'll go and get them some tea,' Lindsey said in an undertone to Tamzin, 'while you cope with this lot. They terrify me!' She turned and hurried down the billiard-room.

Tamzin turned towards the open porch, where Mrs Lillycrop had just dumped her new twins in Mr Lillycrop's already loaded arms so that she could extract one of her numerous young from where it had most astonishingly stuck itself (beneath two prostrate older ones) and at the same time smack Hydrangea because she wouldn't stop screaming very loudly.

'You shut up now, immediate, our Hy, or else I shall smack yer again,' she said crossly, drawing out the squashed one with her spare hand as easily as a conjurer drawing rabbits from a hat. Tamzin couldn't see that it mattered as much as all this about the screaming, considering the noise the gale was making, besides the united uproar of the new twins and an unidentified child, at present eclipsed behind the others.

'We're all going to be drownded!' this hidden one was wailing very lustily as Tamzin, remembering she was the parson's daughter, set forth to welcome the new refugees.

'Would you like some hot tea, Mrs Lillycrop? Good

evening, Mr Lillycrop – not that it is. Wouldn't the children like to come and get warm and dry beside the fire? We've got some beds and things upstairs. Oh dear! How wet you all are!'

'We're all going to be *drownded*!' shrieked the small one in the background.

'Vicar said as we was to come here,' Mrs Lillycrop said with a voice of tragic melodrama. 'Water's in the front door. That's what we're wet with; it ent raining any more. Oh my! I won't arf warm your pants, our Ariadne, if you don't leave off hollerin'. Of course we shall all be drownded if you go on like that! Come along now, all of you, and I'll get you dry, and then you shall all have a nice sip er strong tea.'

'– *drownded!*' roared small Ariadne; then, 'I want a biscuit in my tea!'

They began to crowd towards the chairs Snowey had put ready, Tamzin holding the hand of a very small fair boy whose name she believed was Jupiter, but he was never referred to by any other term than 'our Ju'. Mr Lillycrop bore up well under his ferocious twins and a bundle of mixed bedding; the eldest daughter Minerva carried a sleeping child of about eighteen months old, and the boy Ur heaved along another perhaps a little older or more probably a twin.

'Shouldn't never have got here without Vicar and Goldeye and them,' remarked Mr Lillycrop, very loudly because of the twins. 'Most everybody else's down to the lifeboat. Ent yer got their dummies on yer, Ma?' he asked his wife.

'Course I got 'em; in me bag. Stands to reason. But I ent got nothing to dip 'em in till I finds me tin of syrup.'

'Here it is, Ma!' said Minerva, feeling in a sodden pocket.

Mrs Lillycrop reached for the tin, prising up the lid with a thumb-nail. She dunked the two terrible rubber dummies soundly into its contents and popped them, oozing golden syrup, one, two, into the howling open mouths of her new twins; and immediately there was silence. Such a silence that the gale seemed all the louder, stronger, and wilder.

Then suddenly up went a wail from Ariadne. 'I left me teddy-bear! Oh, Mam! I left me teddy-bear!'

'Shut up, our Arry, or I shall spank yer! You'll start the twins off again, see if you don't.'

'Perhaps someone else has brought the teddy,' said Tamzin consolingly, lifting the child into the chair beside 'our Ju', but Ariadne still sobbed.

The inner door opened and she looked up with relief to see Mrs Clench and Lindsey with the large tea-urn and a jug of milk. Mrs Clench was fussed and anxious, peering down for people's stuck-out feet.

'I had to open a tin, as I ent got no more fresh in the house. You got them cups washed, have you, Tamzin? That's the style.' She banged down the white jug beside the tea-urn on the billiard-table. 'Won't do that green baize no good, that it won't, but it ent no time fer thinking that.'

Lindsey said, 'I wish we had some milk for all these children.'

Mrs Clench rubbed her glasses and replaced them.

'Ee,' she said, 'all them Lillycrop shoal, and wet as a bucketful of eels. Strewth! I wouldn't be in their Mum's shoes.' And she turned and shuffled back into her kitchen.

Lindsey, pouring out tea for Tamzin to take round, was thinking how unfeeling Mrs Clench was being, but she had sadly misjudged her. Within three minutes the caretaker's wife was shuffling back again, and this time she brought a plate of home-made currant buns, a little jar of brightly coloured boiled sweets and a bagful of apples and oranges.

'Fer the children, Mrs Lillycrop,' she said kindly. 'There int enough fer anybody else. And then the sooner we get them wet things off of 'em all, pore mites, and wrap 'em up in blankets, the better it'll be fer 'em.'

'It's mostly only their legs,' said Mrs Lillycrop, 'and Cleopatra's drawers on account of she sat down in it. The whole place is all awash, I'm telling you.'

'I want my teddy!' wailed Ariadne all the louder. 'Don't want sweets, I want my teddy!'

'You shut up, our Arry! Of course you want sweets, don't be silly.' Her mother popped two into her open wailing mouth, causing the child to make a noise like frantic gargling, but soon the ecstatic taste began to assert itself in spite of Ariadne's resistance to it, her sobs subsiding in pathetic little hiccups.

'I don't know what we can do for the smallest children,' Tamzin was saying to Mrs Lillycrop. 'I wonder if the Deeproses would have any milk at the farm if one of us could get there?'

Mrs Lillycrop stared up at her over an orange she was distractedly peeling for a very little girl with large brown eyes, the one called Cleopatra.

'Lor' bless us, Miss, they all takes tea; the stronger the better. An' Father got some biscuits in his pocket what they can dip in it. Now leave off, our Cleo, or I shall cut meself; I ent nearly done yet. No, I can't strip the peel off to look like boats. Anybody'd think we was all at home, the way you carry on, and not arf drownded in the Vicar's billiard-room.'

There was a dull crash and all the lights sank in their glass chimneys.

'We got some more guests to the party, seemingly,' said Mrs Upjohn, who was drying 'our Ju' with the folds of her full skirt, and as she spoke the porch was filled with crowding people, among the foremost being the wives and children of the coastguards.

'To think we'd ever live to see the day!' said Mrs Smeed, as much to herself as anybody, as she bent to pick up orange peel.

'Shut up, our Hy!' said Mrs Lillycrop, though Hydrangea had not, for once, said a word.

The door was forced back again with an effort and a woman in black stepped out into the lamplight from the crowd.

'The sea-wall's gone,' she said, a little wildly. 'The sea-wall's gone, and it's still an hour to high water.'

Then Lindsey's stomach seemed suddenly to turn right over, for the black oblongs of the windows had flashed momentarily into blinding lightness, like a row of white-hot eyes evilly winking, and over the roar and racket of the storm was the duller, deeper growling of the thunder.

Tamzin's hand was on her arm. Tamzin's voice seemed to reach her from a very, very long way away.

'The children ought to be dried and got to bed. Come and help? It'll leave more chairs for these new ones, and Mrs Clench will carry on with the tea. Heaven only knows what we'll do if the lifeboat brings more people in.'

'I'm coming,' said Lindsey, and turned her back upon the windows.

CHAPTER 6

MOONLIGHT UNDER MOONLIGHT

*

To Meryon, pushing into the worst gale in living memory, it seemed a futile thing to send the lifeboat out. More than that, it seemed crazy, foolish, even wicked. Some of the crew were only boys, not much more than his own age but already seasoned fishermen, so early did a Westling boy leave school and launch himself upon the seriousness of living.

It was no good saying any of this, though, to Roger or Rissa or old Jim Decks who battled close beside him through the weather. Not a word would reach them unless it were laboriously shouted and several times repeated, and only something in the nature of an emergency was worth so much endeavour when so much of his energy was already needed to keep him moving in the frenzy of the wind.

They had not very far to go now. He could see the pale yellow windows of the lifeboat house, lit by the hurricane lanterns of the first arrivals and not more than a quarter of a mile distant, so far as he could judge. Old Rissa was keeping up marvellously, because, though a girl of her and Tamzin's calibre was every bit as sensible and courageous as any boy, it was just silly to pretend they were as strong. Tamzin, of course, never did this. She had that kind of crystal-clear honesty which makes some people see things as they really are, and not the way they like to think they are: but Rissa was not like this. Rissa would convince herself and everybody else that black was white if she really believed

71

that it ought to be. Just now, for example; mutely shaking her head and ignoring his offered hand, though why it shouldn't be just as reasonable to share out strength as to share out food or labour, Meryon thought as he drove himself against the wind, he couldn't imagine at all, and he had enough to spare for two.

Roger, a little ahead of them with the ferryman, was trying to keep on the narrow sheep-track without bumping into Jim. It was a good thing, he thought, that the rain had stopped, because the wind alone was enough for anyone to struggle with, without the handicap of sodden, flapping waterproofs and cold rain stinging in your eyes and driving down inside your collar. He was sorry Tamzin had felt it necessary to stay behind because she had a guest. This was just the sort of wild and slightly dangerous enterprise she loved, but it was exactly like her to abandon something she very much wanted, and without any fuss or mock heroics, because she thought she should be doing something else. And that guest of hers; Lindsey something – Roger felt himself off the path and struggled back to Jim and his wildly swinging lantern – she was a rather curious person; very quiet, though perhaps that was only because she had more or less just arrived in strange surroundings. But she gave one a queer impression that she was really quite dreadfully afraid of things no one else very much minded, though nothing on earth would have made her say so. People like that were sometimes just the ones who were most surprising when they were actually faced with danger.

There were only a few more yards to go now, and Roger thought this would be just about his limit. It wasn't only that he was younger than Meryon; he simply wasn't built to the same hard-wearing pattern.

How Rissa was managing he wouldn't like to guess, but, being Rissa, she would certainly have dropped in her tracks before accepting any help. And she hadn't done that, because when he looked over his shoulder he could still see the madly flapping edges of her raincoat in the gleam of Meryon's torch.

The wind out here on this open stretch of shingle was absolutely terrific, and Roger was leaning into it so acutely that he could have dropped his fingers on to the ground. But, for all the screaming, buffeting force of it, there was only one sound now in everybody's ears and that was the almost volcanic roaring and crashing of the breakers on the beach banks.

The great double doors of the lifeboat house were standing wide open, made fast against the snatchings of the gale. Dark figures hauling on ropes could just be seen above the high ridge of the shingle: to those approaching they seemed more like vague shapes seen against closed eyelids than like real people doing a terribly real job of work.

The bows of the lifeboat came slowly into the open as Jim Decks brought his party up to join the others.

'Find a place on the ropes: pull!' he shouted, laying his own rough hands to the nearest gap in the double line of haulers and throwing his considerable weight into the rhythm of the pull.

Rissa was close beside the boat, pulling between Meryon and a fisherman called Walter Goddard. Walter was in the crew and would not be pulling any more when once the boat was out upon the beach bank. He would be standing in the boat with the rest of the crew, facing seawards, waiting for the first crashing breaker to fall across their bows as the lifeboat plunged into the sea.

Rissa strained all her weight upon the rope, her feet

slipping in the shingle as she struggled. The boat was moving faster now, gliding down the runway to the sea. The white paint on her sides gleamed weirdly in the patchy lantern light, her bluff bows moving high against the dark ragged sky. Rissa could feel the hard tight twist of the rope through her leather gloves. She pulled so strongly that she slipped down on to one knee, but she wasn't going to have it thought that her weight had made very little difference, especially after what Meryon had said about physical strength. That was the worst of being a girl: you knew you weren't really much use when muscle was wanted, and if you weren't particularly brainy either, what were you?

Roger found himself next to Hookey Galley, who was also one of the crew. Hookey had moved his hands along the rope a little way to give Roger room, but otherwise he showed no signs of recognition. Not that he showed any sign of anything at all, Roger thought, noticing the sharp hatchet profile above the stout padding of the kapok lifejacket, but then these sea-going people never did, except on downright festive occasions. You could never tell whether they were hot or cold, scared or indifferent, tired or fresh; often not even whether they were pleased or angry. They kept their feelings to themselves. Just now, Roger thought, hauling so hard that the rope tore the skin of his hands, if anyone had been able to see Hookey's face, without the background and the weather, they would never have known that he wasn't working on his nets around the Point, and with nothing ahead of him more exciting than his dinner.

Rissa, glancing up a moment later, suddenly found she was the only one doing any pulling. The crew were climbing into the lifeboat, their yellow oilskins shining dimly with a sickly tint against the darkness.

'Now for it!' Meryon shouted, but his voice reached her as a dull yell, wind-strangled, in the commotion of the breakers on the shingle.

Again, all her strength was drained into the hauling-rope, and now they were so close to the sea that the spray was flung into her face and in her mouth, open for quick rush of panting breaths. Rissa swallowed, vaguely aware of the cold sharp salt taste, and leaned her weight the harder. The tide was very high. She didn't remember ever seeing it quite so high before, and it was still some time before high water.

This time she stopped when the others stopped, and watched what they were watching. She supposed that immensely high dark wall which raced towards them must be an approaching wave, considering where it was; but really it was past believing, as towering as that. In fact the whole thing began to seem so impossible that Rissa almost felt vaguely unreal herself, until the wave curled dizzily over and crashed like crystal dynamite below her straddled feet.

'NOW!' yelled a man with a megaphone whom Rissa couldn't see, and again all hands were straining on the ropes. The great wave was sucking backwards, shifting tons of pebbles with a noise like an earthquake, as the boat began to move again. Now they were on the sharp slope down into the sea, and the sea was very close. The boat was moving faster, faster – she was moving by herself. The hauling-ropes had been flung off, the haulers standing back and watching, leaning into the wind and the spindrift. The lifeboat gathered speed and rushed past them, roaring over the shingle and down into the black wild sea with a plunge that sent up shooting dead-white fountains at her bows.

Someone grabbed Rissa's arm, dragging her bodily

The lifeboat rushed past them, down into the
wild black sea.

up the beach bank. Where she had just been standing was the curdled, tumbled foam of another breaker.

'Come on out of it!' shouted Jim Decks. 'Can't do no more now.'

'Where's Roger?' Rissa shouted back, then saw the dim shape of him with Meryon on the beach beside her.

Roger was watching for the lifeboat, his eyes screwed up, straining into the wind and darkness for a glimpse of her white hull among the toppling seas. But already she was swallowed out of all sight as completely as if she had been rolling on the bottom.

Jim was fussing them back up the shingle banks to the lifeboat house. He was shouting something, but no one could be quite sure what it was. They were all half-running up the steep loose banks with the wind gone mad behind them and the tall seas crashing on the pebbles with a noise beyond believing; then suddenly from the dark shadow of the lifeboat house went up a clear green light, soaring into the gale like a lost shooting star and turning white as it soared.

'What is it, Jim?' yelled Rissa, running on before the wind; but did not properly hear his short reply until, reaching the half-shelter of the building, he repeated it.

'Verey lights, gal. Looks like they want to recall the lifeboat.'

The chief coastguard Mr Grumbitt stood pressed against the open door with others who had helped to launch the boat, finding here the slight protection from the storm's fury that he needed for sending up the Verey lights. The faces of these men looked strangely dramatic, splashed with bold upward shadows cast by lanterns on the floor. Mr Grumbitt slewed his narrowed eyes round from staring into the darkness over the sea and looked at Jim.

'Just had a message to recall her. Vessel they've gone out to has run aground off Dymchurch. Crew all taken off by breeches buoy.'

'Ar,' said Jim gravely, staring into the wind's eye, his face screwed up like a bulldog's. 'I doubt they'll have seen yer signal, the sea being what she is.'

'Not seen it?' Rissa asked anxiously. 'Why not, Jim?'

'If you wuz out in that lifeboat, gal, this minute, what you'd be looking for ud be the next sea coming, and not back shorewards, hope of signals.'

'We'd have had the message through before she sailed,' the coastguard said, 'but so many lines are down, they had to try several roundabout ways before they got it through to us.'

Roger shouted into Meryon's ear, 'They'll send up more lights, won't they?'

'Look,' said Meryon, nodding, his rough black hair whipping wildly on his forehead, because he found this more bearable than the rattle and flap of his sou'wester, unless it was actually raining. Roger and Rissa glanced round and saw Mr Grumbitt slipping a new cartridge into the Verey pistol.

'No reply from them,' he was saying. 'We'll try again while they're pretty close.'

The report of the pistol was smothered at birth by the gale, and flung away on the wind with the tenuous wraith of smoke from its muzzle, but everyone saw the soaring, arching, green-turning-white ball of pure light, like a small moon thrown into the darkness.

Then, as if encouraged by this tiny bright adventurer, the real moon broke clear away from the storm-littered clouds, riding high and radiant with a floating cloak of stars. Suddenly, the sea and shore-line stood out before the watchers. Rissa gasped. Roger and Meryon opened wide eyes despite the cold inner touch of the fingers of the wind.

'Look!' was all Rissa could say.

'Roaring rum runners!' said Meryon.

Roger said nothing, but his mind went racing to the sea-wall and the village and the grazings, for the tide was high above the highest mark they had ever known it reach before, and the whole sea under the white moonlight was a range of towering, melting mountains; white-topped like any other peaks, but terrifyingly mobile, as mountains when the earth was young and hot, and great hills ran like water.

The men showed no emotion, looking at the glinting chaos as one might look at a bucketful of herrings.

'She's showin' her teeth,' remarked the old ferryman, at the top of his voice but casually.

'Dirty weather,' agreed Charlie Deeprose, who farmed the Harbour Farm.

'No reply, still,' said the chief coastguard, peering under his sou'wester.

'Can you see her?' Rissa asked Roger and Meryon, but they shook their heads, staring blankly at this demented English Channel which, only that morning, had been as a pool of heavy dark-grey silk.

'I doubt us'll get back, same way as us come,' said Jim Decks, speaking to Charlie Deeprose at his side against the door. 'I'll lay th' ole sea-wall must've gorn, Char.'

Charlie nodded. 'Just what I was thinking.'

'Not get back?' shouted Rissa, but only Meryon heard her. He cupped his hands to his mouth and said clearly in her ear, 'There's the track to Castle Farm. That shouldn't be under, I think.'

'It's much higher than anywhere else,' Rissa agreed. 'That and the farm itself.'

'And the castle,' Meryon said.

Old Jim picked up his lantern, and the shadows round it shortened, bobbing downwards. He jerked his head at Rissa and the boys. 'No call to stay on here. Thur ent no knowing whur us'll fetch up, see, afore the morning. Now, get tacking.'

Roger said, 'And not see the lifeboat come back, Jim?'

'She ent replied, have she? Then she ent seen the signals, see? I'll lay she's a sight too busy keeping of her head to the sea, ole young un; an' what's more, you can't do her no good with propping yerselves up again the lifeboat house. We-ell then, up with yer anchors and let's get navigating home. Me an' Char here, we reckon th' ole sea-wall's most prob'ly gorn. We're going to make fer Castle Farm.'

'If we can get there we can probably get right through to the road,' Roger said.

'Soon see,' said Jim briefly, stepping out into the full gale and immediately assuming a backwards angle about five times more acute than that of the Leaning Tower of Pisa.

The others followed, with Charlie Deeprose in the rear, nodding a good-night to the men who stayed behind.

'He's thinking of the early milking, or even whether his cows are in danger from the water,' Roger thought, wishing the brim of his sou'wester would not beat so deafeningly on his singing ears.

Meryon was still bare-headed, his usually wavy hair streaming straight out ahead of him in the moonlight, like the black peak of a close-fitting cap. Rissa was trying not to run; her knees were bent as if someone were pushing her from behind. Jim and Charlie sat back comfortably on the wind and let it do the work of walking for them. They merely lifted one foot after the other, judging the angle of their list with nicety, according to the variations of the storm.

They had only to breast the first high shingle bank to see the desolation on the grazings. There they lay, acre after acre under water, shivering white like moonlight under moonlight.

'Cor, dammit, darn take it!' said Jim Decks, stopping in his tracks. Then, 'Jumping gin bottles!' he said, and strode on faster.

'My cows –' began Charlie Deeprose, but didn't add what everyone else knew already. And it wasn't only the Deeproses' cows. Rissa's mind at once became tormented with anxieties about the three ponies. There was her own chestnut Siani, whom she kept at Castle Farm. If Mr Merrow had her in the home orchard she would be all right, for Castle Farm stood higher than all the land around it. But if he had put her with the ewes, down on the castle grazings, or, worse still, on the levels ... If he had done this, then Rissa just couldn't face the thought of what might be happening at this moment.

Then, of course, there were the two vicarage ponies, Banner and Cascade. If the vicarage was all right, the ponies would be too, she supposed.

'How high is Westling Vicarage, Jim?' she yelled, half-running close beside him, their sea-booted feet moving in and out like pistons in the lantern light.

'Wodjer mean, how high?'

'I'm thinking of the ponies – the water –' It was an effort to speak, the wind snatching away one's words when they were barely half-formed.

'Higher'n what we are, gal. All right iffen the stable ent blown orf of 'em.'

'See those lights?' said Meryon. 'Castle Farm.'

'Mrs Merrow,' said Roger thankfully. 'She's still up. She'll have the kettle on the hob.'

'Probably something on the table,' said Rissa hopefully, clutching the frantic flappings of her raincoat.

'I can do with it,' said Meryon, 'whatever it is.'

Then suddenly the moon had gone and there was darkness. Rissa glanced up and over her shoulder in time to see the sky split in half above the sea as if a sword had slashed it, spilling liquid lightning blue as sapphires.

'We got it coming,' said Jim Decks when the drumming of the thunder had subsided. 'This lot ent nothin' but the beginning, mates. We got it coming, surelye.'

CHAPTER 7

BLIND LEADING THE BLIND

*

BECAUSE of the abundance of the Lillycrop children, Tamzin and Lindsey had offered themselves as nursemaids to the six youngest, thus leaving Mrs Lillycrop with only the four elder ones (who were fairly well able to look after themselves, as well as help with the young ones), and all her rescued possessions to sort over and drape about the Institute to dry.

Mrs Smeed and Mrs Upjohn were also helping with babies and children brought in from other flooded cottages, and Mrs Clench had stripped her own beds to help with the provision of dry blankets; for now there were more than thirty refugees, distributed between the Mission Hall and the Institute, and, for all Tamzin knew, more in the vicarage as well.

There was little that anyone could do to help these homeless people, except provide them with warmth and shelter and sympathy, and hot sweet drinks to glow in their chilled stomachs. Tamzin and Lindsey wished they could have made their six small charges more comfortable, but all they had to work with was the big bare upper room and the dwindling pile of clean but scrubby blankets. No pyjamas, no pillows, no sheets, not even any mattresses. And even the six camp beds were not available as these were in the other upstairs room, reserved for the very old people.

Up here, close under the sloping roof, one seemed so much nearer to the thunder. Tamzin couldn't be sure, sometimes, which was the loudest: the rain,

beating on the roof-tiles with a noise like tearing canvas;
the wind, ravening over the village like hungry wolves;
or the thunder, so loud and frequent that it might have
been resurrection day for the world's accumulation of
old sheet-iron.

At first, when the storm was newly burst upon them,
Lindsey had been almost paralysed with fear. Or was it
fear? Not rational fear, she was certain, because it was
always the thunder that melted her spirit inside her;
never the lightning, in which the danger lay. She was
also most terribly afraid of showing her fear to Tamzin
and the others. She was deeply ashamed of it, for, as
usual, she was the only one among so many who seemed
to care about the storm as much as this. No, not quite
the only one, for the very small boy 'Ju', whom Tamzin
was trying to settle in his blankets, was crying bitterly,
his little hands pressed tightly over his ears, his dirty
fingers dark amongst the brightness of his hair.

True, Lindsey's own immediate charge was crying
too, but not because of the thunder.

'I want my teddy-bear! Gimme my teddy; I ent got
my teddy –'

Lindsey was utterly unable to concentrate on the
teddy-bear.

'Sh! Ariadne; you'll wake the twins.'

'I don't wanter shush, I want my *teddy*!'

What was the child saying? Oh, the teddy-bear, of
course; still the teddy-bear. Wasn't that what she had
been crying for before, ages ago when the thunder had
made a sort of short double crack just over where the
fireplace was? Or wasn't that ages ago? Time seemed
to be all anyhow. It was smothered by the thunder, and
so was Lindsey's mind, which didn't seem to obey her
any more but worked vaguely and jerkily like some old
machine that needed oiling.

The elder child Minerva watched the scene with detached but curious interest, propped up on her elbow in her blanket flea-bag on the floor-boards. She watched Lindsey push a hand down into her pocket and withdraw a little model stag.

'Sh! Ariadne. Here! I'll lend you this little stag.'

The child pushed it away, screaming louder for her teddy. Minerva waited for the last thunder-clap to fade into the storm-roar before she leaned from her blankets to say helpfully, 'That ent no good. She won't give over, not without her teddy.'

Lindsey looked across at her, neatly parcelled up between the dummy-sucking twins and thumb-sucking Cleopatra. What was that she was saying? Why did people have to speak to her at all when her mind was so remotely abstracted, tuned-in to the movements of the thunder . . .

She got up from kneeling beside the sobbing Ariadne and went across to Tamzin, who was attempting all in vain to keep the small boy covered in his blankets.

'Let me stay with Ju for a bit, Tamzin. You try Ariadne. She's screaming for something she hasn't got – you might know what to do.'

Lightning filled the bare room with livid brightness and Lindsey jumped. The small boy rocked on his knees and held his head in wide-spread fingers.

Tamzin stood up wearily, looking down at him.

'All right, but don't you think you ought to fetch his mother?'

'No,' said Lindsey. 'I can manage.' And she knelt down on the rough fold of the blankets, suddenly sure of it.

Five minutes later Tamzin looked across the room at her and Jupiter, for surely the boy had stopped his crying? Not that it was at all easy to distinguish any one sound from another in all this fearful racket, but, yes, he had stopped crying. He was curled down peacefully on his jacket pillow, and in one of Lindsey's hands were both his little ones. Her other hand was gently moving round him, tucking in his tumbled blankets.

'Gosh!' said Tamzin to herself, wishing she had seen how Lindsey had achieved this seeming miracle. Most curious it was, too, when almost anyone could see that

Lindsey had achieved this seeming miracle

poor old Lin was simply shaken rigid with the fear of thunder herself. Well, thought Tamzin, picking up her pocket-compass which Ariadne had thrown down in passionate rejection, if this is a case of the blind leading the blind, I'm all for it.

All were quiet, except for muffled hiccups from little Ariadne, when the Vicar looked in on the shadowy scene upstairs some twenty minutes later. Tamzin was standing on a blanket-chest carefully lowering the wick of the last of the two hanging lamps, and Lindsey was looking out of the seaward-facing window, shocked into stillness by the revelations of sudden moonlight. She turned as Tamzin's father came inside the room.

'I don't seem to be able to believe it,' she said shakily, half-laughing because the thing seemed so absurd. 'The village looks as if it were floating.' There was no need to speak softly because of the clamour of the wind.

'I think we all feel rather like that, but it's very real: terribly real to people whose houses are flooded.'

'But the water's everywhere!'

'Let me see!' said Tamzin, stepping down from the blanket-chest and going quietly to the window. 'Jumping gin bottles!' she said, with Jim Decks's exclamation. 'What about Rissa and the boys? Are they back from the lifeboat, Father?'

'No, not back at the vicarage. But Goldeye says they will have made for Castle Farm. We tried to phone the lifeboat house but couldn't even get through to exchange.'

'The lines are down,' said Tamzin.

'I should think practically everything that was ever up is down,' said Lindsey wonderingly.

'I've been sent to relieve the garrison,' said the Vicar. 'You've to come back to bed, both of you. You seem to have completed a very good job here.'

'Except for Ariadne,' said Tamzin, suddenly yawning. 'We keep thinking she's asleep and then she wakes up crying again.'

'I expect it's the thunder,' said the Vicar understandingly. 'She'll soon doze off now it's passing over. I haven't heard a clap for quite five minutes.'

'It isn't that,' Lindsey said, astonished suddenly to discover that she hadn't noticed whether the thunder were passing over or not. 'She left her teddy-bear behind.'

'I've got an old one somewhere in my attic,' Tamzin said with swift inspiration. 'You could bring it back for her, Father – if we really have to go to bed.'

'You really have,' said her father. 'And straight away. Come along down and get your coats on. The road's under water as far as our garden wall, but Thomas Upjohn's waiting with his dinghy, and he says he thinks the worst of the storm is nearly over.'

'I must go and look at the ponies before we go to bed,' Tamzin was saying anxiously, following her father to the door. 'Is the water anywhere near the stable? Have you noticed?'

'It won't be near the stable,' said the Vicar, 'until it's been inside our kitchen. Mother went out twice during the evening to see if the ponies were frightened, but she said they were all right.'

Tamzin was peering down to see her way on the stairs.

'I expect that's because of all the hay and straw up in their loft,' she said. 'It must have dulled the noise for them a bit.'

In the long billiard-room the air was thick with steam and tobacco smoke; faces floated vaguely in the midst of it like lilies on a misty pool. Clothing, rugs, and blankets hung across between the lamps, and you had to duck if you didn't want a cold wet corner slapping in your face.

Outside, beyond the snatching crash of the door, they had to be particularly careful, Tamzin and Lindsey found. One false step, playing into the ruthless hands of the wind, and they would be floundering in the sliding water that had, so surprisingly, turned the road into a river in the space of less than two hours. It was strange, scrambling into Thomas Upjohn's dinghy in the middle of the village main street. Rather like a dream, Lindsey thought, in which suddenly you discover you have your blue pyjamas on, and all the people with you have turned into pigs.

'Hold tight!' Thomas was shouting, just like a bus conductor, Lindsey thought again incongruously, but she held on tighter than she had ever held on in any Surrey bus.

'Is it deep, d'you think?' she shouted to Tamzin, who was hunched down against the wind, beside her.

Tamzin shook her head.

'Can't be – very. It isn't half-way up the doors.'

'Deep enough,' bawled Thomas. 'No monkey tricks.'

No one answered. As if they weren't a hundred times too weary for any monkey business.

'I do hope Rissa and the others are all right,' Tamzin shouted, her head nodding to the strokes of Thomas Upjohn's oars.

The Vicar said, 'They will be. They're with Jim.'

'You carsn't do nothing, no-how,' said Thomas philosophically, and rowed on, slowly, down the village. The gale raced past them so that they seemed to be going as fast as witches, but they had only to raise their eyes into the wind and see the pallid houses in the moonlit water to know that they were going slower than a plough-horse.

The boat grounded by the vicarage garden wall and Thomas helped his passengers step upon dry land.

'I'll be coming back in about three minutes, Tom,' said the Vicar, showing only a little in his voice of the weariness he must have been feeling.

'Pack it up, Vicar,' advised Thomas, spitting out into the wind-ruffled water. 'I'll lay you done yerself about all in. Carsn't do more nor what you got the strength for, choose how.'

'I'm not really very tired,' said the Vicar, cheerfully committing perjury in the good cause, 'and we must go round and see how they're doing at Harbour Farm before we finish.'

Tamzin and Lindsey were already battling their way around to the stable. The water hadn't reached it, as they really knew it couldn't have, and the two ponies were quiet in their boxes, munching hay. Tamzin sighed with relief.

'So that's all right! Now the teddy-bear. I've got to get it quickly before Father goes away again.'

The cold wind leaped at them from round the corners of the house and stables, knocking them sideways, but now they thought nothing of it. So used were they becoming to it, that almost it seemed as if gales were the only weather that they had ever known; the fair, still days seeming so remotely far away that they might have belonged to another life, a long, long time ago.

In the vicarage, Tamzin's mother came to meet them anxiously.

'You must be simply exhausted!'

But Tamzin, kicking off her wellingtons, hurried on across the kitchen.

'Don't let Father go for just another minute, will you? I have to get something from upstairs.'

'Oh, well,' said Mrs Grey, smiling uncertainly. Then, suddenly calling after her: 'You'll be careful not to wake Diccon, won't you?'

'What? In all this storm racket?' Tamzin called back. 'But I'll be careful.'

Her mother smiled more certainly. 'What a welcome

for you, Lindsey! I'll take your things, and you sit right down and have a plate of this hot soup.'

'It's a nice sort of welcome,' Lindsey said. 'It makes me feel as if I'd been here years and years. And, oh, it's tomato soup! My favourite thing out of everything, I think, except strawberries and cream.'

'I've got it!' said Tamzin, running through the hall with a surprising fund of energy. 'It only has one eye and no ears, but she'll probably not notice in the dark. Here you are, Dad! Don't forget to give it to her, whatever you do, will you? Oh my! Tomato soup! I didn't know I was so hungry.'

'What ages and ages ago it seems since we were playing murder in the attics!' said Lindsey suddenly, looking at Tamzin over her steaming bowl.

CHAPTER 8

'THERE WAS A SEA-WALL...'

*

So tired was Tamzin at daybreak that she hardly noticed Lindsey's hand shaking her shoulder, or heard Lindsey's voice saying her name.

Lindsey was tired too, but when you are a stranger in a strange land you sleep lighter than the natives, and she had woken just as the cold, colourless first glimmer of the dawn had filmed across the attic bedroom. It had been a queer awakening. The first impression she had, apart from the sudden realization of not being in her own bed in a distant Surrey farmhouse, was a strange awareness that something had stopped happening. It was rather like the feeling you have when a clock has stopped in the night. For hours you have slept through all its steady ticking noise and never even noticed it, but almost the very moment it has stopped, you are awake and wondering what has happened.

Lindsey had pulled herself up on to one elbow, so tired that her body seemed like lead, listening to the silence that so strangely seemed to swing inside her ears. Then she knew what it was. The storm had blown itself out. For hours she had slept up in this roof-level eyrie, hardly aware at all of the roaring and rattling and banging, or the rocking of the high attic bedroom in the wind. But now it had stopped, and its stopping had woken her, and she saw that the first touch of day had made the seaward window pearly.

She was out of bed in a moment and shaking

Tamzin gently on the shoulder; then a little less gently.

'Tamzin!'

Others were about the house already. She could hear movements downstairs. Movements as clear in the unaccustomed silence as pebbles dropped in a deep calm pool.

'Tamzin!'

On second thoughts, Lindsey suddenly decided, the silence wasn't really so absolute as she had thought, because humming through it all was the sustained roar of distant breakers that had not subsided with the wind.

'Tamzin!'

There was a deep sigh, lifting Tamzin's green eiderdown, and then a slow movement of waking limbs, a grunt, and Tamzin's eyes were open. She shut them again at once.

'It's still night.'

'Not really. The daylight's just beginning.'

Tamzin yawned.

'The storm's stopped,' said Lindsey. 'There isn't a breath.'

'Good gracious!' said Tamzin, struggling into wakefulness. 'So it has!' She was rubbing her eyes, sitting up, yawning again, her tawny plaits tousled down her back. 'I say! I wonder if the others have come back? And if the lifeboat's in? I'm getting up.'

'Someone's already up, downstairs,' Lindsey said, feeling about for her clothes in the milky darkness of the dawn.

'Father and Mother, I expect,' said Tamzin, hunching her legs from underneath the bed-clothes. 'Probably been up all night. We might even find all downstairs full of refugees.'

'Or water,' said Lindsey, unbuttoning her pyjama-jacket.

'Can you see anything from the window?'

Lindsey went across and looked, stripping off her jacket as she did so.

'Not really. Only a sort of greyness.'

She clicked the catch across and slid the lower half of the window up.

'That's better,' said Tamzin, drawing in a deep slow breath. 'Awful having to sleep with it shut, but you simply have to, with a storm like that.'

'What a *row* the sea makes! Just like an underground railway.'

Tamzin's head came out through the top of her vest.

'Better get your clothes on. It's colder than you think.'

Downstairs there certainly were refugees, but as one of them was, most providentially, the vicarage daily help, Mrs Briggs, all other things seemed to be so much easier to cope with. Mrs Briggs was the kind who makes light of troubles, bulldozing cheerfully through any that could not be dealt with by her own peculiar strategies or by circumnavigation.

She was leaning over the long black range, pouring oatmeal into the vicarage's largest saucepan and stirring it the while, as Tamzin and Lindsey came into the lamplit kitchen.

'Good morning, Mrs Briggs; what an enormous lot of porridge!'

'An' what if it is now, Tamzin? My eyes aren't any bigger nor all them hungry stomachs in the droring-room, as they say. Reach us the salt, there's a ducks. I bin and almost forgot it again.'

Lindsey took the salt-cellar from the cruet on the dresser near her, passing it to Tamzin.

'How many people, Mrs Briggs?' she said.

Mrs Briggs turned and favoured her with a shrewd inspection before answering, 'Well now, strike me down if I hadn't clean forgot you was coming! Forget me own name I will one day, so Mr Briggs say. How many? Well, there's a great lot too many for one pair er hands, so you can stir this porridge while I lay brakfuss for 'em. And Tamzin, you better fetch me in a bucketful of coal. I sent yer Mum and Dad to bed about three, and if anyone disturbs 'em they'll have me to reckon with.'

'Oh, all right, Mrs Briggs. But we've got to see to the ponies –'

'They won't hurt for five minutes. Now you get on and stop arguing.'

Tamzin retreated into the scullery regions with the empty bucket in her hand.

'Have Rissa and the boys come back?' she called over her shoulder. 'Is the lifeboat in, do you know? I say, are our refugees lifeboat ones, Mrs Briggs?'

Mrs Briggs ignored all this, flapping about the kitchen in her large black plimsolls assembling things on a tray and asking Lindsey how she had slept, between grumbling complaints about her old feet killing her, and her legs not being what they used to be.

Tamzin staggered in with the full bucket, the shovel brandished in her other hand to balance the heavy weight.

'Mrs Briggs –'

'And shouting like that!' said Mrs Briggs, rattling down a handful of spoons upon the tray. 'But you don't catch me so ill-mannered as to shout an answer.'

'Sorry, Mrs Briggs! But are they?'

'Now, how would I know?' said Mrs Briggs maddeningly, slamming down the big black kettle close to the porridge saucepan and making Lindsey jump.

Tamzin sighed. Mrs Briggs was definitely not up to her usual form this morning. She supposed it was owing to worry and lack of sleep, but in any case the sooner they got clear of her bows the better. Peering into Lindsey's saucepan she said, 'It's thickened. Come along to the stable.'

'Shall I leave the spoon in it?'

'Yes, it's wooden. It won't hurt it, and I dare say it adds to the flavour.'

Tamzin was reaching for matches on the mantelpiece, then for a hurricane lantern from the dresser-top. Lindsey levered the glass chimney up for her to light the wick, clicking it down again as the yellow flame licked along the wick's edge.

'And another thing,' Mrs Briggs was saying as she spooned tea into the pot, 'don't forget to put your wellies on. You never saw such a mess as you made on my carpet, going down there in your sandals yesterday.'

'All right, Mrs Briggs – Come on, Lindsey. We shan't need coats just for the stable.'

Outside the back door they paused a moment, surprised at the gain in strength of the daylight.

'Looks as if we shan't need the lantern, either,' Lindsey said.

'We shall in the stable. Golly, Lindsey! Look! Smiling Morn's shop window's broken, and his chimney gone.'

'We saw the chimney'd gone last night. It's really Mr Goldeye, isn't it?'

'Yes, but we call him Smiling Morn because he's so despondent. *She* isn't, though. Jumping gin bottles!' said Tamzin suddenly, looking over the wall.

Lindsey came and looked too. 'The water's absolutely everywhere!'

'Hasn't the roof gone off that cottage? It's rather dark to see.'

'It does look awfully like it. And just look at the things floating! Lots of apples and stuff.'

'Another two yards and it'd have been in this garden.'

'It's up to Smiling Morn's doorstep.'

'There's a tree across the street.'

Tamzin turned and looked up to the vicarage roof. 'But all our chimneys are there. All the windows too, I think.'

'The gale hit the other side,' said Lindsey.

'Ponies first,' said Tamzin, setting out across the tennis lawn. 'I say, doesn't it seem peculiar to be able to walk upright?'

'Yes, and not have the wind roaring in your ears and making your eyelashes tickle.'

'Stable looks all right,' said Tamzin hopefully, approaching the yard. 'Except for a few tiles off. And – Crikey! Look at those buckets we left outside last night; they're right across the yard!'

'And there isn't a leaf left on those plane trees,' Lindsey said.

'Oh, gosh, it's like a sort of abomination of desolation. I don't dare to think what we shall see everywhere when it gets really light.'

Tamzin shot the bolt of the stable door, calling quickly to the ponies as she did so.

'Hallo, ponies; it's only me!'

The door swung open and they went inside, sighing their deep relief at finding all in order.

'We'll put them out now,' said Tamzin, 'and clean up in here later. You can take Banner. Here's his halter.'

'What a relief they're all right,' Lindsey said from Banner's stall.

'Cascade's a bit nervous, though. Quiet, pony, quiet now!'

Lindsey was pulling the halter over the small pony's head. 'Poor Rissa; isn't her Siani somewhere on the Marsh?'

'Yes, but Mr Merrow's awfully good and reliable. I expect he's got her in their orchard and she'd be all right there; it's so high. You'd better let me take Cascade out first. He hates Banner going out in front of him.'

Lindsey held the little bay pony back from the door. 'I expect that's because you had him first, and he's much older.'

They led the ponies out into the grey morning and across the yard into the paddock. Banner pushed himself against his halter, trying to get ahead. His rich bay neck wrinkled up beneath the halter-rope as he tucked his small black muzzle into his chest, rolling his eyes backwards at Lindsey to impress her with his spirit.

'He thinks he's no end of a little horse!' she said, smiling her amusement at him.

They watched the ponies roll and wander off, sniffing at the wet grass. Then they turned and suddenly noticed the vicarage from a new angle.

'Tamzin! Look at your roof!'

'That's almost all the ridge tiles! And what could have made that hole? As if a bomb had dropped through it.'

'You *have* lost a chimney-pot. Perhaps you'll find it in the other attic.'

'Must have a quick look round before breakfast.'

On the west side of the house, where all the windows were double because of the gales, they found every outer one broken, the glass lying in shattered fragments in the flower-beds.

'And the greenhouse!' Tamzin exclaimed sadly. 'What will Mother say?'

'There's nothing left at all but the framework.'

'And look at all her plants! Oh, I say!' Tamzin bent to straighten shattered chrysanthemums and cyclamen where they had been flung among the debris. Suddenly she stood up, a mangled azalea in her hand, and stared in amazement at the top of the high garden wall. 'Lindsey! They've absolutely *gone*! The Seaward Cottages. You used to be able to see the tops of them from here. Look, there isn't a thing!'

'That'll be who your refugees are,' guessed Lindsey, following where Tamzin was now running: round the corner of the house and into the front garden where the wall was low enough to look over.

'Not a stick!' said Tamzin, aghast. 'Not even a dust-bin or a chicken-coop left.'

'They'd be the first things to go. But fancy whole cottages!'

'They were only made of wood, but it was a whole row of them,' Tamzin said.

They stared in silence at the strange blank space where the Seaward Cottages had stood. To Tamzin it was like suddenly discovering that her right hand wasn't there, or that no sun hung in a cloudless sky at midday.

'We could see half across the village from the attic,' suggested Lindsey. 'It's light enough for that, now.'

They turned and ran in through the front door,

meeting Mrs Hobbs from Seaward Cottages in the hall,
her newest baby in her arms.

'Oh, I'm so glad you're alive!' exclaimed Tamzin
fervently. 'It was awful seeing no cottages, and no one
telling us beforehand. Are all the others here too, Mrs
Hobbs?'

'Mostly all, thank God. But Granny Thurlow she
just clean died of fright, poor old soul. And Willy
Sweatman he only lived an hour after they dug him
out from under the chimbley what'd fell.'

'Oh, dear! And we never heard any of it.' Tamzin
bent her head in shocked amazement. 'Oh, Mrs
Hobbs, do you know if the lifeboat's back?'

'Well, I know the crew ent, and that's a fact, for
Willy's brother George was in it, and so was Mrs
Thurlow's boy, and they'd have been in here be now,
looking for their famblies, surelye. Perhaps she come
in at Folkestone or Dover, see, on account of the Marsh
being under water.'

'Yes,' said Tamzin, 'of course, perhaps she did,' and
followed Lindsey quietly up the stairs.

Lindsey was saying, 'Are all your windows always
like this, or is that the storm too?'

'Like what? Golly! You can't see a thing out of
them! I never noticed.'

'That's what I meant,' said Lindsey. 'They're sort of
like bathroom windows, all dull. But in a single night!
Would that be salt or sand or both?'

'Both, I should think,' said Tamzin. Then, 'I've got
some binoculars here,' as they came into her room
again. She lifted them from the top of her chest-of-
drawers and took them to the landward window, which
she opened with an upwards thrust. 'Well!' she said
weakly. *'Well!'*

Lindsey said, 'You don't need binoculars to see

how awful it all is. Looks as if a hurricane's swept over it.'

'I expect it was a sort of hurricane. You never really knew all this as it was, Lin, but you see all that great stretch of water – right from the sea? That was all land yesterday; green levels full of sheep. What a mercy it isn't summer, because there'd have been thousands of sheep then. Now I expect they're mostly up in the hills for the winter.'

'Is that Cloudesley Castle? Stuck right out in the middle of the water?'

'Yes. And look, Lin, there was a sea-wall right down there, and all was dry this side of it. Now, you can't even see where it was!'

'And almost all the village is standing in the water, and people going about in boats. Like a sort of English Venice.'

'To think we slept through most of it! I say, Lin, there's a boat coming out past Cloudesley Castle, and I'll bet you anything that's Rissa and the boys rowing. You look.'

Lindsey took the binoculars and held them to her eyes. 'It does look awfully like them, especially Rissa. You can hardly mistake her Egyptian-looking hair.'

'Oh good, I hope it is! Now the other window.'

They rushed across the room to the seaward window, leaning out of it.

'It's nearly up to your garden.'

'And it ought to be more than a mile away,' Tamzin said, screwing sideways to see the distant lifeboat house. 'Nothing but water. There's the lifeboat house, and the beach bank it stands on, but it's cut off on all sides. I shouldn't think anyone would ever get back from it now, except in a dinghy or something.'

'She's sure to have put in somewhere else,' said Lindsey, 'if she saw what had happened.'

'She couldn't have seen, except in patches of moonlight, perhaps.'

Lindsey was sweeping the glasses slowly along the far line of towering storm-waves, beyond the sheet of quiet flood-water.

'The sea looks simply awful still, but there isn't any wind at all.'

Tamzin said, 'It always takes ages to settle down, once it gets properly stirred up.'

'Think of being in a boat in all that!'

'I dare say some people are.'

'Tamzin! Isn't that a boat, over there, out to the east of the river mouth? I say, mightn't it be the lifeboat, perhaps?'

'Let me look!' Tamzin took the glasses, directing them off Dunsmere Sands on the other side of the river. 'It isn't properly light yet . . .'

'Someone else thinks something's out there,' Lindsey said, leaning from the window to see around to the Hard. 'Five men . . . one's looking through a telescope . . . looks as if he might be Jim Decks.'

'Golly, but you're right!' said Tamzin suddenly, holding the binoculars rigid. 'And it is the lifeboat. You couldn't mistake her shape, and her white hull whenever she comes up on a wave-crest. Now she's gone again behind a big sea.'

'It jolly well is rough,' said Lindsey. 'All white and frothed up. You can even see the points of the waves on the horizon, without glasses . . . Tamzin, did you know your rose pergola is down? It's all across the drive.'

There was a stumping noise on the stairs, which was Diccon coming up.

'Can I look through those glasses, Tamzin? Hallo,
Lindsey. Did you know there's been an awful gale and
all the place is flooded? Oh, and Mother says it's
breakfast.'

CHAPTER 9

LOAD OF BAD NEWS

*

BREAKFAST in the vicarage dining-room that morning was like a restaurant in a rush hour. The fifteen refugees from the vanished Seaward Cottages were crowded round the big table, which had been extended to its full length by the insertion of its extra leaf, and the vicarage family and Lindsey waited on them all, eating their own breakfast in snatched moments in the kitchen.

Mrs Briggs stood at the scullery sink washing relays of plates and knives under a running tap, because the vicarage only had twelve of everything, while the Vicar kept the kettle boiling for the pots and pots of tea he was successively making and serving to the morning-saddened guests.

Mrs Grey was everywhere, now ladling porridge for Tamzin and Lindsey to carry, now slicing bread for Diccon to take into the dining-room, now seeing that Mrs Briggs's cup was filled, or talking to one or other of the homeless ones whose plight seemed to her as dreadful as if it had been her own house and possessions that had gone with the wind of the storm. She was also worried about Lindsey.

'It really is too bad that this should have come just when you were visiting us,' she said in her motherly way. 'I should think you'll always remember the welcome Westling gave you!'

Lindsey was drying a handful of knives, one by one. 'I shall *want* to remember it. I wouldn't have missed it for worlds – if it had to happen at all, I mean. It's simply dreadful for everyone, I know.'

'Is there any more sugar?' Tamzin asked, coming into the kitchen with two empty bowls. 'There's no more in the dining-room.'

Whenever there was a spare moment Tamzin and Lindsey dashed upstairs to look out with the binoculars. They always slowed up to pass the study door quietly, however, because in here were reverently laid three who had lost their lives in the violence of the night. There were the two from Seaward Cottages and one poor seaman so badly battered that none could put a name to him.

Through the north attic window Tamzin and Lindsey kept the progress of the Castle Farm dinghy under close observation until finally, on their third look-out, it was no longer visible, being hidden among the houses of the village.

'Soon be here now,' said Tamzin. 'The lucky blighters. Fancy having breakfast with Mrs Merrow – no one ever cooked as she does – as well as all the excitement of the launching.'

From the south window they watched the lifeboat, tossing about off the Harbour mouth like a red-and-white cork in a mill-race.

'She must be meaning to come up the river, when the tide's right,' Tamzin said.

'It's awful the way she just vanishes, as if the sea had swallowed her,' Lindsey said, peering frantically through the binoculars.

'But she always bobs up again. There she is! See?'

Before the breakfast was finally cleared away, Jim Decks had arrived at the vicarage with a load of bad news.

'It's the Deeproses got it wuss, sir. Least, not them, as

you might say, but their animals. Ole Char he spent the night waist deep fighting fer to save 'em, but his place is lowish, you know. They lorst near a hunnerd sheep and six outer their seven cows. Nor not a chicken saved, Char say.'

The Vicar nodded sadly. 'That is very hard, Jim: if anyone really worked and saved to build up a farm, the Deeproses did. Oh dear, I am so sorry!'

'And there ent a boat in the Harbour what missed it; no, not one. Six of 'em's clean gorn, sir. Mebbe find un up to Dunsford, if we ever claps eyes on 'em again. Our Jimmy's *Stormy Petrel*'s lorst her mainmast, and Wally's *Samphire*'s broke away from her moorings and laying on the mud-bank. Then there's the Post Office, Vicar; they got it all right. There wuz packets er tea and stuff floating out the door as I come sculling by. 'Fact I brought one along here.' He placed a damp lump out of his pocket upon the kitchen table. 'Thought it'd mebbe do more good in some pore soul's stummick nor what it would feeding fishes, and us can allus square up with old Fred arterwards.'

The Vicar nodded again, having no words to express his sorrow for the village.

'And ter cap all,' went on Jim, twiddling his old peaked cap in his rough hands, 'there's that dawg er Hookey Galley's. You wouldn't know, Vicar, I reckon, but he bought it cheap orf a Dutchman what come in a day or two back. It were one er them squorshed up fighting dogs, what Hookey took a fancy to, see. Narsty tempered too, and er course Hookey wouldn't mess about with no quarantine, law or no law. And now the tarnation animal's lorst track of.'

The Vicar looked at him thoughtfully. 'I shouldn't think we need worry much about that, Jim. Most probably the poor creature's drowned.'

'D'you mean he might have rabies, Jim?' Tamzin asked.

'We-ell, I wouldn't say that, gal, but Wally an' me, we thought he didn't look too special like.'

Lindsey said, 'Perhaps he was just miserable about leaving the Dutchman.'

'Mebbe, ole young un, mebbe. An' we got many a wuss trouble to worry over, so we have.'

Tamzin said, 'You've seen Seaward Cottages, Jim?'

The old man looked at her from under his craggy brows.

'No, gal, that's just what I ent seen; no more ent anyone this morning. I hear you got two corpses out on 'em, Vicar,' he added to Mr Grey in a low hollow voice, meant to convey respect for the dead.

The Vicar assented gravely. 'Willy Sweatman and poor old Granny Thurlow. As a matter of fact, Jim, I'm not a little relieved to see you this morning, as it happens. There is a third body, you see – rather difficult to identify after its battering in the storm – and some of us had fears it might be you; especially as it was found quite near your ferry-hut.'

'You don't say!' said Jim, marvelling. 'Well, p'raps I better look-see at it?'

They went across the hall, old Jim striding in his sea-boots and the Vicar walking lightly as was his habit. Tamzin and Lindsey saw them pass from sight into the study, and they paused a moment at the foot of the stairs to hear what Jim might have to say about the unknown one.

There was a moment's silence, and then came Jim's voice, clear and carrying as always with the fishermen. 'No sir! That ent me!'

A shadow of a smile flickered over Tamzin's face.

Out in the scullery a sudden cheerful noise went up.

'It's them!' said Tamzin, pausing on the third stair.

Mrs Briggs's voice came through the open kitchen door: ' – All that noise! With corpses in the study and refugees in the droring-room –'

'Sh!' said Tamzin, as Rissa and Roger and Meryon burst into the hall. 'Come along up to the attic; we've been watching you coming from up there. We've simply heaps to ask you.'

'We've heaps to ask you too,' said Rissa, taking the stairs two at a time.

'There never was such a flooded village,' said Meryon.

'And are there really corpses in the study? How many?' asked Roger, charging after them along the narrow landing.

'Did you know the lifeboat's waiting off the river mouth?' asked Lindsey. 'We've been watching her too.'

Meryon had paused to look in wonder at the opaque landing windows through which nothing could be seen.

'Gosh, no; is she really? She'll be coming up on the tide. I say, Tamzin, you'll never be able to see a thing through your windows again.'

'The north ones are all right. Oh, Rissa! How about Siani? Was she in the orchard? Lindsey and I kept thinking about her. And what about all the Merrows' sheep?'

Coming into Tamzin's attic now, Rissa answered, 'Siani's all right, thank goodness! But only because of Mr Merrow's marvellous weather sense. She was right out on the levels with the other ponies and the sheep, but Mr Merrow said he didn't like the look of things –'

'What he said was,' said Roger, leaning out of the south window, '"I says to meself, that fare to blow middling smartish."'

Rissa nodded. 'Yes. Can I see through those glasses? Thanks! So he sent Mike and Joseph to fetch her and the farm ponies home, and then they went out again and drove all the sheep up into the hills.'

Meryon said, 'They told us people laughed at them – you know, the way they do at chaps who go and sit on hilltops and wait for the end of the world and all that – but they didn't lose a sheep, not one.'

'The only Marsh farm that didn't, I should think,' Tamzin said. 'The Deeproses lost all theirs, and six cows too. I say, there are still people on the quay, looking out at the lifeboat with telescopes. Can you see her, Rissa?'

'Yes, now and then. Isn't the sea jolly rough!'

'Let me look!' Roger said.

'What is one pair among so many?' said Meryon shrugging, and he went to lean out of the north window and marvel at the village in the water.

Roger was saying, 'Did you ever hear about Sea-born Sarah, Tamzin? At Castle Farm?' He juggled with the glasses.

'Oh, yes, I think so. She was Mr Merrow's grandmother, wasn't she? And she was born in a sailing ship.'

'Yes, and brought up in it too, till she met the William Merrow of those days and married him.'

Rissa burst in. 'She came back – last night. Both Mike and Mr Merrow saw her, Tamzin. They said she was standing at the gate, between the farmhouse and the sea, right through the storm.'

'I wish they'd woken us!' said Roger. 'All the ghosts you ever come across were seen by other people. I can see the lifeboat now! I say, doesn't she plunge about.'

'But the extraordinary thing is,' said Rissa, her elbows on the window ledge, 'the Merrows didn't have the smallest bit of damage. Not even a window broken.

or a single creature lost. Mr Merrow said Sea-born Sarah came back to protect her old home.'

Tamzin stared at her, marvelling. 'Well, they certainly must be the only place on the whole Marsh that didn't lose *some*thing. And Mr Merrow never imagines things, either. Oh, how I wish I'd been there!'

'Well, we were, and we never saw her; so I don't suppose you would have, either.'

'I think I would like to have,' said Lindsey suddenly, gazing at the wide flood-water with unseeing eyes.

Meryon's voice came from the north window.

'I say, it's almost like it used to be, hundreds and hundreds of years ago, when the sea was right up to Winklesea and Dunsford.'

'You know what old Jim always said,' Tamzin reminded him. '"The sea will always come back to her own."'

'The old pessimist!' said Meryon.

'He was jolly well right,' said Roger. 'You can have a squint through these things now, Meryon. I think I can see better without them.'

'You don't know how to use them, my lad, that's what it is.'

Rissa was now recounting mouth-wateringly what Mrs Merrow had cooked and served for breakfast, but all were crowded round the south window watching the frenzied dancing of the little lifeboat on seas as high as houses.

'– and after that there was thick yellow cream to spoon into our coffee.'

'Gosh!' said Tamzin enviously. 'And we only had lumpy porridge and bread and marmalade.'

'It wasn't lumpy,' said Lindsey, defending it. 'I ought to know. I made it.'

'You really only *stirred* it.'

'Peace, my children!' said Meryon, focusing the glasses. 'It's the stirring that makes or mars the porridge.'

'We never stir ours at home,' Lindsey argued. 'We do it overnight in a slow oven.'

'Funny thing,' Meryon said thoughtfully after a while, 'the way the lifeboat's behaving. You'd think she'd keep her head on to the seas, so heavy as they are, but she keeps going about ... almost as if she were looking for something.'

'Oh? She wasn't when I was looking,' said Roger. 'Are you sure?'

'Of course I'm sure. I'm –'

There was such a long pause here that the others began to stare at him doubtfully. Then Meryon suddenly lowered the glasses, turning to Roger and Tamzin with a queer slow look.

'She's gone over – I saw her – right over.'

'What? The lifeboat? Capsized?' Roger stared incredulously.

'While I was looking at her. She just went right over.'

'Oh Meryon! In that sea!' Tamzin was aghast. 'Let me look!'

'The men have seen it too,' said Rissa, leaning out to see the group upon the quay.

Everyone turned towards the Harbour, and there they saw the watchers, running.

'She was broadside to the wind,' Meryon was saying, 'and a big sea caught her. Now why should she have done that? Why didn't she keep her head to the wind? I don't make it out.'

'They're going to get ropes,' Tamzin said, her eyes on the running fishermen.

'For life-lines?' asked Lindsey.

'I expect so . . .'

'No good putting a boat out, I suppose,' Roger said.

'Nearly every boat in the Harbour's lost or damaged.'

Suddenly, without another word, the five of them turned and raced downstairs.

'Mother, Father, oh, Mrs Briggs! The lifeboat's capsized.'

'Tamzin! Darling! Are you sure?'

'*Capsized*, Tamzin?'

'Oh my! Them pore boys! Whatever next?'

'Meryon saw her. Mother, the men were running for ropes. May we go too?'

'We-ell –'

'Oh, thank you, Mother! Are you coming, Father? We'll have to be awfully quick.'

Everyone was scrambling into waterproofs again.

'You must have your wellingtons!' Mrs Grey insisted anxiously.

'I got me kettle on the boil. You wait two shakes and I'll knock you up a coupla thermoses. Oh, the pore lads! And my Char'd have bin out there too if it weren't fer his having broke his thumb.'

'Do be quick!' begged Tamzin.

'Just a minute and I'll get the brandy flask,' said Mrs Grey. 'And Richard, can you stuff this first-aid box in your coat pocket?'

The first rescue gang had already crossed the river when the vicarage party arrived at the storm-battered ferry hut, but another boat-load was pushing off and they made room for everyone somewhere, wallowing out across the widened river with the water nearly over the gunwales.

Tamzin was shocked at the wreckage and ruin in the little Harbour; boats were piled up on the mud and flung about the Hard like worn-out bath-toys. Fishing gear lay sprawled half in the water, among oars and boat-hooks and boxes. Beyond the high Harbour banks all was water, and the cottages stood with their feet in it, their blank windows like shocked square eyes.

Landing on the Dunsmere side the Vicar's party set their faces to the distant beach, for this was where the easterly drift would toss back the toll that the sea had taken.

'If only,' Tamzin suddenly said, 'Sea-born Sarah had loved the lifeboat as much as she loved Castle Farm!'

CHAPTER 10

STORM-WRACK

*

ON the long Dunsmere beach the tall breakers raced in and reared themselves higher than Tamzin would have believed possible, before flinging themselves down with a crash and a splintering of spindrift.

Another thing that she would scarcely have believed was that men could live in all that terrible leaping water, but men were far out into it, roped into the bowlines of the life-lines, and she and Lindsey and the others were helping with their weight to hold the long swaying lines steady, like human anchors planted in the wet ribbed sand.

Behind them on higher sand one figure lay stretched out face downwards, and the man working over him was Tamzin's father, who had long ago taught himself and his family the skills of life-saving and artificial respiration, because of the watery situation of his parish.

Now and again Tamzin glanced backwards over her shoulder in hope of seeing any signs of success in her father's solitary labour, but always he was swaying in the same rhythmic swing that was of the same beat as a man's breath. Away beyond him was the queer new line of the wind-sliced sand-dunes, their crests now scattered over the flat Marsh fields behind them, and all about the foreshore was the wreckage and flotsam of the storm-wrack.

'Haul away now; steady does it!'

The sturdy voice of the ferryman set his line hauling in. Tamzin and Lindsey and Roger shared this position

'Fifteen still to come'

with him, and all were continuously wet with the
spray from crashing breakers. Jim himself, at the head
of his line, was as much in as out of the water. His
white woolly beard was sparkling with it and his oilskins ran shinily with each fresh onslaught from the sea.

Right out at the end of Jim's line was the young man
Bob Smeed, and with him there was now another man,
from the overturned lifeboat. No one could see who it
was because of the heavy seas that raged along the
shore. It could easily be Jim Decks's only son, Jimmy,
Tamzin realized suddenly, remembering that Jimmy
was a member of the crew. Not that this could have
made the least difference to old Jim, for family ties
were of very small importance to all these men,
compared with the urgency of rescue. The man who
lay unconscious on the sand was brother to Clam
Caister, who was in charge of the next line to Jim's, but
the need to save all lives kept Clam at his post without a
backward glance towards his brother, for there were
many men tossing in the sea, and few to save them.

'I hope it's Jimmy!' Tamzin said fervently to
Lindsey as they hauled the sodden rope in, hand over
hand.

'I hope it's anyone – alive.'

'Only the second,' Roger said. 'Fifteen to come.'

'They'll all come at once now,' said the ferryman.
'God help 'em!'

'Someone on Meryon and Rissa's line,' Roger said,
slanting his gaze obliquely down the shore, but now
was no time to notice any more, for their own man was
in hand's reach, struggling in the water with his burden,
and all hands stretched to help him.

'I got – to go back –' gasped Bob. 'Another man –'

'You get yer breath, ole young un. Never be no use
without.'

Jim was lifting the limp lifeboat man clear away from the water. It was not his son.

'Ole Hookey,' he said. 'Living, anyways, but pr' nigh gorn.'

The shore was now crowding with anxious relatives and friends, and there were willing hands waiting to carry Hookey Galley from the sea. His sou'wester and sea-boots had gone and his wet head hung limply with water running from the nostrils.

Already Bob Smeed was wading back, bracing himself against the stunning flail of breakers, and the wet rope was paid out again, slipping through cold and numbing fingers.

'There's the boat!' Roger said, nodding; and Tamzin and Lindsey saw her, bottom upwards, tossing white and distant on the waves. An oar was flung up on the next breaker, landing near to Lindsey. She dragged it clear of the water and went back to her place on the life-line.

The crew were coming in fast now, as Jim had said they would. Both the other lines had hauled in and put back again and the beach was dotted with the dark groups of first-aid helpers. Tamzin saw an ambulance turn on to the shore from the cut through the dunes to the roadway, its tyres biting a dark double line in the sand.

'Floods can't be very deep this side of the river,' Roger said, noticing it, 'or they'd never have got here from Dunsford.'

'They jolly well are, though,' Tamzin said, wiping a wet sandy hand across her face. 'They must have come through from Dungeness way, I should think.'

'Come on a bit back'ards,' said the ferryman, absently driving them. 'Tide's coming in smartish.'

Tamzin looked at him with sudden compassion. 'You

wouldn't miss me on the rope for a bit. I could go and find out if anyone's got Jimmy –'

The old man's eyes were on the sea. 'Couldn't make no difference, gal. We got a job on. T'ent only our young Jimmy, see.'

It was nearly an hour later that Meryon came across the sand to Jim's line and reported the finding of young Jimmy.

'I think he's all right, Jim; once they get his breathing going. They're nearly all like that; but I don't think Jimmy's hurt anywhere.'

The old man nodded, saying nothing. He was watching the life-line run slowly through his fingers as a new man pushed out into the mad loud water, relieving the exhausted Bob Smeed who had been unwillingly driven home to warm the life back into his chilled body with dry clothing and hot tea.

'I'll take your place for a bit, Jim,' Meryon offered, and Tamzin, looking at him, thought he couldn't be much wetter than he was.

The ferryman hesitated, frowning over the sea with his narrowed blue eyes. The man on the end of the line was lost and then appeared again, diving through a great green breaker like a wall of curling glass.

'Right, son; I reckon you'll do,' he said. 'Watch fer him lifting his hand, then haul in careful.'

'Aye, aye, Jim.'

No one turned to watch the old man plodding over the hard sand to where other men fought for his son's life, kneeling in the storm-wrack under the grass-grown dunes. The life-lines were dark snakes circling untidily where they fell upon the shore; or they were shining silver streamers under the fitful sun whenever the sea threw them into view above the boiling water. Tamzin's and Lindsey's hands burned with the friction of the wet sandy coils.

'I don't know why we didn't think of gloves,' Tamzin said, taking one hand from the line to wipe it tenderly on her sleeve.

'You wouldn't really expect anyone to think of anything much except getting here,' Meryon said, 'when men were in the water.'

'And if we had remembered, we'd have worn them into shreds by now,' said Lindsey.

'Lifeboat's in much nearer,' Tamzin said, shouting over the roar of crashing breakers.

'There's our man!' Meryon pointed, his gipsy-dark face alert under the salty wetness of the flung spray.

'The next wave,' said Tamzin. 'He'll get him on the next wave. Let the line out a bit, Meryon. Look out for that breaker! Now it's in your wellingtons.'

'I'll have 'em off in a minute. Feet've been drowned ages.'

'He's got him!' shouted Lindsey.

'Haul away! Carefully does it.'

Tamzin's eyes watered at the renewed sting of wet sand in raw-rubbed blisters.

'It's Frank Snudding. You can tell by his fair hair.'

Lindsey was blinking too. 'You wouldn't think a man could live a minute in all that.'

Meryon's black hair was plastered wet upon his forehead like thrown Indian ink. He said soberly, 'I think perhaps some of them didn't. There were two on our line we didn't feel very easy about.'

'Here they come!' said Tamzin, her eyes on the water.

'When Jim comes back,' Meryon said over his shoulder, steadily hauling, 'you two ought to go and help the first-aid people. No one's really any use on a rope when their skin's rubbed raw, whatever you'll both say.'

'Why should we say it? We only want to be where we *are* useful.'

Meryon was wading into the surge and swirl of water now, reaching out hands to help the man on the line's end who swayed beneath his sodden burden, the water pouring down from them both, only to dash over them again with a roar of curdled foam as they staggered from the breakers.

Meryon was helping to support the limp weight of the fair-haired lifeboat man; Tamzin's and Lindsey's hands were stretched across the edge of swirling water.

Two women came running down from the higher sand ridge. Tamzin could hear the voice of one: 'It's our Frank! I know it's our Frank, by his hair . . .'

By nightfall of that Sunday, the stricken village had begun to know its losses. In sheep and cattle, poultry, crops, and buildings, these were heavy, for few people had had time to save much from the inrush of the waters. But the village counted these as little compared with the losses of their menfolk, for at sundown, out of the fifteen lifeboat men that had been snatched from the waves only ten had survived, and five more lives were added to the known toll of the storm. Little hope was held out for the missing two members of the crew, but no man was ever counted lost by Westling folk until all hope must be abandoned.

Among the ten survivors there was hardly a man without serious injury due to battering in the tremendous seas off Dunsmere, and it was known that the village would see at least two of its men on crutches before ever it saw them man a boat again. The lifeboat herself lay high and dry, still bottom upwards, upon the sand of Dunsmere, but all the life-line crews had now come wearily homewards, after a long hard day broken only by the arrival of sandwich lunches from the village. They were soaked and cold, and dispirited because of the two that were not found.

In the vicarage sitting-room the Vicar stretched aching legs to the heaped fire and looked across to his wife with tired eyes.

'It's good to be home, Gwenda.'

'It's good to have you all back. Diccon and I've been thinking of you all, and the crew, ever since you left this morning. This is Lindsey's tea, Tamzin, and this is Meryon's. And Roger, you could pass round the toast; it's in the hearth.'

Tamzin balanced the cups. 'I don't know what I'd have done if they hadn't found Jim's Jimmy. Old Jim would never have got over it.'

'Is he going to be all right?' Mrs Grey was anxious, wanting desperately to know all but not wanting young Diccon to hear of things that would harrow his compassionate soul beyond his years.

'I think so, now,' said the Vicar, rousing himself to drink the steaming tea that Rissa passed him. 'We took three hours to revive him. There were moments when I wondered.'

'It must have been a miracle,' said Diccon, marvelling. His sandwich clung, unregarded, like a limpet to the plate that tilted forward in his hands.

'It was a miracle, my son,' said his father, his long lean frame relaxed thankfully in the printed flowery background of his chair, where he looked rather like a friendly telegraph pole reclining in a herbaceous border. 'He was taken up to Dunsford Hospital, by a roundabout route to miss the floods, with all the others of the crew. Jim says he's rowing his wife and several neighbours there this evening.'

Lindsey said, 'Tamzin and Rissa and Roger all took turns with artificial respiration.'

'There were so many,' Roger said.

The Vicar nodded, looking soberly into the fire. 'Not a man came in conscious.'

'Oh dear!' Mrs Grey was distressed. 'If only I could have helped!' She fussed about the room, restless with the sense of inactivity, drawing the cheerful curtains against the falling darkness, adding more logs to the salt-smelling blaze of driftwood, pouring Diccon's milk for him into his squat brown china tankard.

Rissa said, 'Jim was furious because Meryon went in on the end of a life-line, but Meryon pulled a man in.'

Meryon looked at Rissa with angry Siamese cat eyes. 'Everyone else was done in.'

'Oh, but Meryon –' began Mrs Grey anxiously, sitting down again beside the teapot.

'*No*body's told me *why* the lifeboat capsized!' Diccon suddenly wailed. 'And I've asked and asked!'

'Does anyone know yet?' his mother asked, absently filling up cups that Rissa passed her.

Mr Grey leaned to put his empty plate upon the trolley, having scarcely eaten anything at all.

'They tell me that Farley the coxswain made a statement late in the afternoon, when he had recovered enough to be questioned. They lost a man overboard – one of the two we haven't yet found – and Farley put the boat about at once to try to pick him up.'

'I saw it!' said Meryon. 'That's what I saw from Tamzin's window. I said to Tamzin, "Why on earth have they gone about?"'

'You all know what happened after that,' the Vicar said.

'So they never picked up the man?' asked Mrs Grey.
'No.'

'Who was he, Richard?'

'The youngest in the crew, young Billy Gudgeon. A great pity. He ought never to have gone out at all, but they were a man short owing to Gudgeon's having influenza, so Billy insisted on going instead.'

'He was only a little more than Meryon's age!' Mrs Grey was shocked. 'Poor Billy!'

'But they made enough hue and cry about me going out on a life-line!' Meryon was disgusted.

'It's because you're still at school,' Diccon told him with strange wisdom.

'He's right,' Rissa said. 'Because Billy Gudgeon's been at work a year, he's a man and treated like one.'

'And allowed to throw his life away,' said Meryon, 'while I'm supposed to walk about on the shore and keep my feet dry.'

'I shouldn't worry,' said Rissa dryly. 'You never have done what you're supposed to, yet.'

The Vicar shook his head sadly. 'I can't help feeling what a pity it all was; a very great pity, because all so unnecessary. The men were taken off the *Pole Star* before our boat was even launched.'

'If only they'd seen the recall flares!' said Lindsey.

'Or if only Billy hadn't fallen overboard,' said Tamzin.

'No good saying "if only",' Rissa said sensibly, 'or you could keep on going on; "if only the telephone lines hadn't been down," or "if only there hadn't been a hurricane," and all that. What I say is, I think it's jolly marvellous they saved so many alive, in a sea as rough as that was.'

'That's the spirit,' Meryon said. 'Never look backwards.'

Mrs Grey began to collect the empty cups. 'No one's asked me about our refugees.'

'Do you know, I'd absolutely forgotten them!' Tamzin said. 'It seems such years and years since we were here this morning, and saw the Seaward Cottages had gone.'

'Well, so have some of the refugees; to friends and relations in the village and in Dunsford. We've got six left, and Mrs Briggs and I nearly wore ourselves out this morning trying to stop them spring-cleaning the vicarage, but in the end we lost ground and the refugees won. You wouldn't believe how clean we are. Do have some more ginger-bread, Roger, before I clear it away. You still look famished.'

'Oh thanks! I am, even after all those sandwiches and things you sent us.' Roger was always hungry, and needed no encouragement.

'And what about the Lillycrops?' Tamzin asked. 'And the others in the Institute? And have they found Hookey's dog?'

'No dog, so far as I've heard, and the Institute people are nearly all still there. Poor Mrs Clench has had rather a day of it, I'm afraid, minding all those children while the parents salvaged what they could at home. One blessing has been the relief boat. The Mayor of Dunsford sent one down this morning full of supplies: food and blankets and first-aid dressings and all kinds of useful things, besides tins and tins of milk, which were a godsend in view of what happened to the Deeproses' cows.'

'The Lillycrop children,' said Tamzin, speaking from experience, 'don't have milk. They have tea, the stronger the better.'

'And biscuits dunked in it,' said Lindsey.

'They wean them on kippers, I expect,' said Meryon, 'and cut their teeth on beer bottles.'

'The very small one they call Jupiter,' said Lindsey, remembering, 'is *nice*. If I were old and rich, he's just the kind of little boy I'd want to adopt.'

'Tamzin!' exclaimed her mother suddenly, noticing for the first time the hands that helped to stack the tea-things. 'Your hands are simply raw!'

'I know,' said Tamzin, turning them up to look at them. 'All our hands are. It was the wet sandy ropes.'

'You must all come into the kitchen and let me dress them at once. What a state they're in! Why ever didn't I notice them before?'

'There is one good thing,' said Rissa with a sudden cheerful inspiration. 'I don't think we'll any of us be able to wash dishes for quite a while – unless it's Meryon.'

'Even if we could,' Tamzin said, 'it'd still be stables first. D'you know we haven't even mucked them out since yesterday? I never thought I'd live to see the day that we wouldn't do the ponies till the evening.'

CHAPTER II

WINGS OF HIGH COURAGE

*

THE stables were quickly done, with so many hands; and the two ponies, being left out rather later than usual on account of the day's delays, were leaning over the paddock gate in the falling darkness watching the work going on in the light of the hanging stable-lantern. Cascade's long black tongue was lolloping in and out as if he were lapping air, but this was only because of his thoughts of crushed oats and hay and did not deceive anyone into thinking he was on the point of collapse. Diccon's little Banner trotted stoutly up and down inside the fence, whickering continuously in a low gruff voice and stopping every few yards to shoot up his ears and fix his full gaze on the stable, as if hoping that the work might seem nearer to completion from a different viewpoint in the paddock.

'Hasn't it struck you as most odd,' Roger was saying as he forked up the dark patches of soiled straw, 'that no one has so much as said a word about school?'

Tamzin was measuring out the ponies' evening feeds at the corn-bin. 'So they haven't,' she said in a surprised voice, and the old pudding-basin she used as a measure made a dry hissing noise as she leaned and plunged it down through the dull gold deeps of corn.

Meryon, forking bedding in the next stall to Roger, grunted in his don't-you-believe-it manner. 'Not to us, they haven't. You can't really suppose they haven't thought of it, though.'

It was Lindsey's job to help Rissa rack-up with hay

from the loft, and she was standing on the wooden partition between the two stalls that Tamzin used as loose-boxes, pushing down into the racks the forkfuls of airy hay as Rissa poked them at her.

'If the road is under water nearly all the way to Dunsford, and all the village simply standing in it, I don't see how you can go. I say, Tamzin, why don't you have holes in the loft floor just over the hayracks? Then you'd only have to give the hay a shove to fill the racks.'

'Father wouldn't because of Diccon. I mean, he had them boarded up, years ago.'

'How they can send you to school and the boys and me home,' Rissa said, walking under her palm-tree top of hay that softly rustled, 'is by boat, as soon as they think of it.' She screwed up her eyes tightly as she lifted her load to Lindsey, and the light pointed hay-seeds fell on her hair and down her neck.

'Boat? What boat?' Meryon's dank forkful settled heavily down into the barrow. 'Everyone in the Harbour is frantically salvaging and mending, to say nothing of scrabbling about looking for lost oars and masts and sails.'

'I dare say,' Tamzin said. 'But haven't you noticed that even if practically everyone's down with the Black Death – and all those that aren't have broken all their ribs and legs, and it's raining riversful, and there isn't any transport, or anything at all – the first thing they always think of is: How shall we get the children to school?'

'I can't say I have,' said Rissa, strictly practical. 'You want a higher nail for your lantern, Tamzin. It smites me every time I pass under it.'

Roger was forking back the clean straw, its yellow showers falling loosely and lightly under the soft light

from the swinging lantern. He said, 'Tamzin's the one
– you'll see – who'll come off best in this. She'd have to
make a journey every day to Dunsford, but once they've
got us home again everything'll be just the same as
usual for all us three.'

'They're sure to find a boat for just one journey,'
Rissa agreed sadly. She leaned her hands and chin on
her pitchfork handle for a moment, watching Meryon's
last fork-load of fresh bedding straw go down with a
crisp springiness upon the floor of Cascade's stall.

'Let 'em all come!' said Meryon. 'Beds, feeds, hayracks; all in order. Our Hotel Caters for the Customer.
Come to Westling if you want your bed forked over
nightly, buckets in all bedrooms and no thistles in the
food.'

Tamzin said, 'Come on, Lindsey, we're fetching
them in.'

Roger was saying to Meryon, 'You jolly well do
remind me of an advertisement my dad once noticed
in a paper – it was about holiday rooms, you know –
and it said, "running water in all beds."'

Meryon looked at him for a moment, leaning over the
wooden partition, and then burst out into his sudden
deep guffaw.

'They meant bed*rooms*,' said Rissa, bringing the
whole thing briskly down to earth.

'You don't say!' Roger swung himself back from the
doorway and Tamzin came through into the pale-gold
light with the white Cascade, whose nostrils shivered
with deep expectant thrills at the nearness of supper
and sweet hay. Banner was at his heels, dragging Lindsey through the doorway, his stout sides vibrating
visibly to the depths of his greedy whickering. The
ponies plunged their muzzles down deep into their
mangers. Cascade gave a great contented snort, and

oats and chaff flew out at either side of his face, like a bow-wave flying out beneath a boat.

'He always does that,' said Tamzin. 'It's terribly wasteful.'

'Mrs Briggs,' said Roger, his mind directed to the idea of food, 'is making a wonderful big supper. She told me when we passed her in the kitchen.'

'I expect you asked her,' suggested Meryon wisely.

The supper was indeed a masterpiece, considering the extreme difficulties under which all Westling housekeeping was now being managed. Mrs Grey and Mrs Briggs had planned and achieved a menu beginning with kidney soup and sweeping delectably on through three bacon-and-egg pies (with Mrs Briggs's melting flaky crust, patterned in leaves and roses, on them), tinned peas and creamed carrots, to a vast dish of crisp and golden apple fritters (the apple cut in rings with holes in the middle), served with showers of castor sugar, like hoar-frost on a corn-stack.

A great assembly sat down to this meal, for the refugees were persuaded to forget their shyness and leave their private quarters for the supper, and there were the four visiting children as well as the Greys themselves. They all packed round the big table with knees and elbows rubbing, but now and again expanding with deep-drawn breaths as some of their number squeezed out of their places to help with the carrying of plates and dishes. It might indeed have been a very gay occasion, except for the sobering thoughts in everyone's mind of the three who lay dead in the darkness of the Vicar's study; the five more from the lifeboat who now, beneath spread Union Jacks, were laid on trestles in the Mission Hall; and the two who still were not found – floating, possibly, in greeny depths, or even, everyone still doggedly hoped, alive on some distant shore, cut off from quick communication because the telephone lines were all down.

The Vicar had worries of his own, that no one else but Mrs Grey would have been likely to realize, and one of these was the problem of how to arrange for the burial of eight parishioners, with the churchyard half under water and the greater part of the village street too deep for wading except with tall sea-boots. There were not small boats enough available for the carrying of eight coffins – ten, perhaps, if the two missing lifeboat men should be recovered upon the next flood tide. And a burial, the Vicar pondered as he served the crisp round fritters stacked before him, a burial is not a thing one can put off until the waters drain from street and churchyard.

He was also worried about the unknown man: that third one in his study whom no one had identified. A stranger, thought the Vicar, undoubtedly a stranger staying in the village: though not at the William the Conqueror Inn, for Mrs Gudgeon the landlady had herself rowed round to view the corpse and said it was none of her acquaintance. Possibly, the Vicar pondered, they might have had a stranger at the Sea Serpent, the other inn at the farther end of the village, though this was unlikely at such a time of year. However, he thought, he probably wouldn't be able to rest until he had found out about this, so after supper was finished he decided, he would scull himself up the street in the little leaky dinghy Jim Decks had left for his use and make inquiries. He said as much to Mrs Grey as soon as he could get her to himself for a moment, while everyone else was crowding in and out clearing the table, just like Ashford Junction in a rush hour.

'Oh Richard, must you really?' She looked up at

him with the concerned expression of one who knows she has no control whatever over a loved one. 'After such a day? You must be absolutely weary; surely to-morrow would do as well?'

The Vicar smiled at her, the wrinkles deepening at the corners of his eyes. 'You know to-morrow's never any good to me.'

And she did know, of course, and said no more about it, except such things as, 'I'll light a hurricane lantern for you, it'll be easier in the dinghy than a torch. Oh, and put your warm overcoat on, won't you, Richard? It's really much colder than one thinks.'

Lindsey, coming into the kitchen with a couple of empty dishes, saw the lit lantern and the Vicar pulling on his coat.

'Oh,' she said, suddenly remembering something, 'do you think you will be going past the Sailors' Institute?'

'Past it, yes,' said the Vicar, 'but not into it. Do you want something there?'

'Oh yes!' said Lindsey. Then, thinking she was probably going to sound very silly to anyone who couldn't know how much it mattered, she added, 'At least, it isn't really terribly important, I suppose. It's just a little model of a stag. I lent it to Ariadne when she was crying in the thunder, but she didn't really want it. In fact she threw it away, only I didn't look for it at once, and then –'

'You forgot it till too late,' said the Vicar. 'I understand perfectly. How will it do if I drop you at the Institute and pick you up on the way back? That all right, Gwenda?' He turned to look at her inquiringly.

'Oh – I suppose so.' Mrs Grey didn't like the idea very much. It didn't fit in with any of her motherly instincts. 'Don't any of you people ever get tired at all?'

'Not till we've done everything we've set our minds on doing,' said Meryon. He was passing through the scullery with a tray of glasses and a jug.

'It only makes you tireder, being stopped from doing something you've got terribly on your mind,' added Tamzin as she folded one end of the long tablecloth, with Roger muddling himself up over the crease-marks at the other end.

Mrs Briggs, banging about in the scullery, had still heard every word and added her opinion in tones that managed somehow to be at the same time loudly affectionate and fondly disapproving.

'You'll none of you talk so barmy when you gets to my time of life. More likely to be putting up your feet sensible and laying back when you can grab the charnce.'

Mrs Grey was helping Lindsey into her brown tweed coat, slipping a torch into her pocket, and some biscuits for the hosts of the Lillycrop children.

'I should give them into Mrs Clench's keeping; not straight to the children, or they're sure to eat them in bed, after their teeth have been cleaned.'

'And have a sleepless night, with tummy-ache and crumbs in their nighties,' added Rissa practically.

Tamzin pushed the folded tablecloth into the dresser drawer.

'Don't forget to see if Ariadne's sleeping with my old teddy-bear still. If she's thrown him away I think I'd rather you brought him back. I've had him so many years. And besides,' she added, in case further explanation might be thought necessary, 'I think Diccon rather likes him.'

'I won't forget,' said Lindsey. She pulled her long

brown plaits out from inside her coat, delving into her pockets for her gloves as she followed Tamzin's father to the door. 'It really is much colder,' she said. 'You wouldn't think it possible.'

Outside the back garden gate the water lapped the roadside. The little dinghy was faintly visible in the clouded moonlight, drawn up on to the grassy verge among the heaped ruin of the storm. Lindsey's wellingtons scrunched nastily in rotting apples and vegetables, where the slowly receding water was beginning to dump the flotsam and jetsam of the gale. The Vicar stood his lantern in the dinghy's bows and Lindsey helped him push her off into the water, their feet slipping on the squashed refuse as they braced them for the effort.

Then they were afloat, and the Vicar was rowing with the neat deliberation that was characteristic of him; no rush, no visible effort, the oars dipping and feathering as precisely as for an exhibition of style.

Lindsey, in the stern, was saying slowly, 'About Seaborn Sarah –'

'Yes?' said the Vicar.

'I wonder – what do you think? Do you suppose she's really true?'

The Vicar rowed four immaculate strokes.

'Yes,' he suddenly said. 'I think she might be. You remember – "More things are wrought by prayer than this world dreams of."'

Lindsey pondered, looking at the dark high walls of cottage fronts, made darker by the squares of lighted windows.

'D'you mean the Merrows' prayers? Or Sea-born Sarah's?'

'Perhaps in this case,' said the Vicar, 'it was both.'

The shining windows made undulating reflexions of

themselves upon the dark water, and once the dinghy cleft her way through the centre of a mirrored bedroom window, splintering the bright square into a thousand broken sequins. The Vicar nosed her gently in to the Institute steps and Lindsey straddled herself ashore.

'I'll be back here for you in about twenty minutes, I should think,' he said, pushing off with an oar against the steps.

'More things are wrought by prayer than
this world dreams of'

'All right,' said Lindsey. 'I'll be waiting.'

There was no one in the long dark billiard-room as she went through, her torch casting a moving oval on the floor, for all the grown-up refugees were working sixteen and seventeen hours a day at salvaging their property. Lindsey opened the far door and, standing at the foot of the narrow stairs, could hear the sounds of knives and forks on plates from within the Clenches' kitchen. So they were having supper, Mrs Clench and

134

Albert. It seemed a pity to disturb them, just for a model stag and half a pound of biscuits. Lindsey shone her torch up the bare wooden stairs and decided to creep up quietly on her own. There was no sound from the upper rooms, surprisingly, which indicated that the children were most probably all asleep. Perhaps, thought Lindsey, tiptoeing up the stairs, they had all stayed awake so long the night before (what with the wind and the thunder and the strangeness of their sleeping place), that to-night there was no possibility of keeping awake.

The stairs creaked, as stairs always do whenever you most urgently desire them not to. But, once asleep, small children rarely wake to noises as soft as these were.

Lindsey creaked on, up the stairs and along the high dark landing, pausing at the door of the children's dormitory to shade her torch with rounded fingers before gently turning the handle and going inside. The light shone through the edges of her fingers, outlining them with rosy pinkness, and was filtered down to move along the floor in clouded bars. No sound came from the cocoon-like rolls of children sleeping on the floor and Lindsey crept along between them looking for her stag. It was unlikely to have been tidied away, she sensibly reflected, for everyone was far too busy now to have any time for anything but the bare essentials. It would be somewhere in the room.

She paused a moment, coming to small Jupiter, for whom she had found a sense of warm protection, and was surprised at herself for her motherly relief in seeing, by the filtered torchlight, how carelessly he lay in tranquil slumber. But the stag was not there.

Again she paused at Ariadne's place, and smiled a little to herself to see one leg of Tamzin's teddy sticking queerly from the rolled blankets. She wondered whether Tamzin would be pleased or disappointed when she told her. Ariadne herself looked like a fallen Seraph with one thumb lost to the hilt in her rounded little mouth.

Lindsey moved on, feeling oddly like the Lady with the Lamp, but the stag was not with any of the children. She thought about other likely places, then remembered that there really weren't any in this bare upper room; only the window ledges and the chest where the emergency blankets were kept. On the chest were only a candlestick, a pile of clothes and a bag half-full of biscuits, beside which Lindsey left her own bag, thinking this better than to disturb the two at supper downstairs.

Moving quietly back down the other side of the dim room, her torch still carefully shaded, she found the little stag lying on its side upon the second window-sill, its splendid antlers looking helpless, hanging vaguely into space. With a quick joyful gesture Lindsey reached her spare hand for the stag, tucking him carefully down into her pocket, then turned back thankfully towards the distant open door. The thought uppermost in her mind was relief that all had been accomplished so smoothly without waking or disturbing anyone at all. Then suddenly her heart stood still.

The room was very dark, with only the small pool of broken torchlight, but there was no mistaking the astonishing and faintly frightening fact that her path between the sleeping children was now barred by a large and silent dog. To Lindsey this fact was as shockingly incongruous as if she had found a sheep in the vicarage kitchen. The Clenches hadn't a dog, and neither had the Lillycrops. Then how had this one got into the children's sleeping quarters? She herself had left the bedroom door open, of course, while she looked around for the stag, but she had shut the outer one all right, so the dog must already have been inside the Institute building. Perhaps it had crept in unseen while Mrs Clench was shaking mats or carrying ashes to the bin.

'Good dog, good dog!' she whispered anxiously, afraid of waking the children, but the dog didn't move from her pathway. She took a cautious step forward, heard a low sinister growl and moved back again uncertainly. She began to look warily around her, lifting her hooded torch to see if she might get back down the other side of the room, stepping carefully over the rolls of sleeping children. Yes, she decided, that would be perfectly possible. But still she was uneasy, not liking to move in case the dog should bark and wake the children. She was also (though she wouldn't admit it to herself) very frightened because of the silence and the stillness of the way the dog just stood there. And it was so odd, so very odd, to see a dog in that place at all.

Carefully, she let her shaded torch rest on it. It was a fairly big dog, probably a bull-dog; its eyes looked red in the torchlight. She stared at it and suddenly saw, to her mounting horror, that it was slavering and drooling at the mouth. In a flash her mind went back, and she was remembering the old ferryman talking in the vicarage kitchen about the loss of Hookey Galley's dog – the one that should have been in quarantine for rabies, and wasn't – and how Tamzin had asked if he had thought the dog was sickening for rabies, and he had answered that he and the other man at the inn had not much liked the look of it. Lindsey was in a dilemma; if ever there had been a situation calling for quick action, this was one, and she didn't know what to do.

The overwhelming temptation, of course, was to get out as quickly as possible, down the other side of the room, and then hasten to the kitchen for the help of Albert Clench. But if she did that, mightn't the dog be roused by her movement into sudden attack? It would be simply terrible, she thought desperately to herself, hearing her heart-beats like a water-ram, if *she* were the object of attack. But surely (even though fear made it difficult to face this), wouldn't it be so much more horrible if an attack were made upon the smaller sleeping children? Lindsey thought agonizingly of little Jupiter: so small and helpless and afraid. But what to do?

The dog remained; statuesque and menacing. Lindsey too remained; frightened, uncertain, and desperately wondering how long Tamzin's father would be in coming. The sudden hopeful idea that it might not be Hookey's dog after all (in which case it could hardly be rabies, because of the disease being extinct in this country), she pushed reluctantly aside, for so much evidence pointed to the contrary.

She would probably have stood there indefinitely in the dark silent room, unable to face the thought of any action, hoping feverishly for someone – anyone – to find her, if the dog had not slowly begun to swing its drooling head and sniff the floorboards. Lindsey watched it, horrified. Her eyes noted clearly the details picked out by her shadowed torch; the red quivering nostrils, and the small pool of saliva slowly spreading on the floor. But her legs and arms were wooden, not responding to her mind's clamour that something must be done, and done very quickly.

Then the slow click of heavy claws on floorboards jerked her sharply to her senses. The dog was moving, growling softly as it shuffled, and Lindsey's eyes dilated with the horror of the sight of one small sleeping bundle being nosed and slavered in the dimness. Still she stood there, wooden as a figurehead, frantically praying that it wouldn't be small Jupiter, racking her terrified mind to remember just where Jupiter had lain. And then suddenly the high frightened scream of the little child rang out, piercing through Lindsey's dulled senses with the cold shock of a sword-thrust, and she flung herself across the space between.

With the first closing of her scared hands upon the collar of the dog, her fear ran from her. Now she was no longer wooden, sick with fright and cowardice. Now she was pulling the slobbering hot terror down the dark room between the roused and screaming children. She could feel the warm saliva running round her wrist and the steamy breath against her knees. The door was a million miles away, but now she didn't care. This was how soldiers felt in battle, when the first craven cowardice had left them: lifted on the wings of high courage and elation.

The blunt claws of the dog were scraping on the floorboards, and it was growling queerly, past the tightened collar as she pulled it.

If only, she thought, the children would stop screaming. All was safely over now, and she was, most miraculously, almost at the door.

Someone was running through the billiard-room, but Lindsey now was through the doorway and out upon the landing. With a great surging rush of relief she turned and shut the door behind her. But in doing so she had freed one hand from its grip upon the collar, and the dog, seeing its chance, screwed round and sank its teeth into her arm.

CHAPTER 12

UNSPOKEN DANGER

*

WALKING a little uncertainly in at the vicarage back door, Lindsey slipped her feet out of her wellingtons and allowed Mr Grey to take her arm, as if she had been an invalid, and help her through the kitchen.

'Well, now –' began Mrs Briggs, looking up from her stacking of tumblers on the dresser shelves and immediately scenting trouble as a cat will scent a mouse. But the Vicar was already through into the hall, shepherding his slightly doddery charge and saying, 'Just a little accident, Mrs Briggs; these things will happen.'

Apart from an odd sensation of throbbing, Lindsey's arm was not particularly painful, bound up as it was with Mrs Clench's quickly torn-up old sheeting and a pad of cotton-wool, but Lindsey herself felt very strange and vague, as if walking about in someone's dream, or on a cloud. And when they were in the lamplit sitting-room and everyone staring suddenly at the way the Vicar held her other arm, and at the white queerness of her face, all she could think of to say was, 'I found my stag. And, Tamzin, Ariadne's sleeping with your bear.'

The Vicar steered her gently to a chair which Meryon was swiftly vacating for her, while asking with sudden concern, 'I say, is she hurt?'

Lindsey sat bolt upright in the deep and comfortable chair, afraid to settle back into the softness of the cushions in case she drifted altogether out of consciousness, so slender was the hold she felt she had upon it.

Strange it was, but rather nice, to hear the Vicar telling of her meeting with the mysterious dog. It was almost, Lindsey thought vaguely, as if it were all a tale about someone else, especially the bits about her coolness and great courage; because of course she had actually been downright paralysed with fear and much more concerned about her own safety than with that of the Lillycrop children. At least, at first she had been. She did remember now being simply torn with horror at the sudden thought of little Jupiter. But nearly everything that happened after that was very hazy in her mind; which was a pity, because from what they were all saying now it seemed it had been rather gallant, and there wasn't much about herself that might seem gallant, Lindsey thought with mild regretfulness.

The Vicar was saying, 'Mrs Clench has washed the place with antiseptic and done it up quite well, and she gave her some hot sweet tea to help the shock, but of course we've got to think now how we can get her to the doctor. The sooner the better, I think, in view of the dog's health being suspect.'

'If only it hadn't been now!' exclaimed Tamzin, who sat with both the cats crowded on her lap. 'No boats, and the road all flooded right to Dunsford. However will you do it?'

'Do you mean straight away, Richard?' Mrs Grey was feverishly thinking over all the possibilities as she gently padded extra cushions down behind Lindsey's upright back, wrapping her coat around her knees because the warmth was good for shock.

'I think perhaps we ought.' The Vicar also was for the moment at a loss. 'We don't know, of course, that the dog has the disease. Clench has it fastened up in his net-shed for the present, under observation. I've asked him to look after it well and to write down any details he notices about its behaviour. But meanwhile, I suppose, we should assume the worst and act on that, in case there is any infection. And I think, where the bite is infected, the less time one loses, the better.'

'If only we had the telephone,' said Mrs Grey, 'and could ring up Doctor Hargreaves.'

Rissa threw back her heavy hair. 'Isn't there really any boat at all? Not one?'

'Not one that isn't more or less badly damaged,' said the Vicar. 'This old dinghy of Jim's that we're using: we had to bale her out all the way home. She wouldn't do two miles.'

'Couldn't we use the ferry-boat?' Roger said. 'Though of course that's leaking badly too, but we could keep on baling out.'

'We might have done, if it were there,' the Vicar said, slowly shaking his head. 'Don't you remember Jim said that he was taking his wife and three neighbours to stay with relatives in Dunsford, so that they'll be handy for seeing young Jimmy in hospital?'

'So he did,' said Tamzin. 'And that he wasn't coming back until the morning. Oh dear! It just would work like that.'

Meryon suddenly said, 'I expect you'll think this a crazy idea, sir, but at least it is an idea. There'll be boats in Dunsford, because the harbour there is more sheltered. They won't need them so urgently as we do, not being cut off from the mainland the way we are.'

'Don't forget there's no telephone,' said Rissa.

Meryon ignored this. 'I could perfectly well swim the distance, wading where it's shallow enough, and get a boat sent back with the doctor. The only real snag, I think, is the time it would take.'

'There must be a better way than that,' said the Vicar, being careful not to say 'less dangerous', for he knew this would only make Meryon all the more determined, he being a descendant of the notorious pirate Tonkin Fairbrass and endowed with all the mad adventurousness of his ancestor. 'And a quicker one,' he added, thinking this would more effectively squash the reckless project, and of course he was right, for what was the use of high adventure if the desired end were not thus achieved more quickly and effectively?

'Father!'

The Vicar's thoughts were interrupted by the urgency of his daughter's voice. He glanced at her questioningly.

'Father – that net-shed at the Clenches' – is there an *inside* door to it, from the house, as well as the one to the yard?'

'There is, I believe. Yes, of course, I know there is. Why?'

'Oh, *Father*! Then it's all my fault! I let the dog in. I never thought about an inside door, but when I was getting some coal for Mrs Clench, and it was raining and blowing so hard, I saw the dog huddled against the net-shed, and I let him inside. I knew it might be Hookey's, because I hadn't seen it before and I know all the village dogs, but it looked so miserable and I didn't think there could really be anything in what Jim and the others thought about the rabies – you know how down on Hookey they always are, and – Oh, but if only I'd remembered to tell someone! I suppose Mr Clench just opened the door for something, and the dog slipped through in the darkness. Oh, *Father*!'

'Anyone might have done it,' said Rissa, stoutly loyal. 'You can't leave any creature out in weather like that. And I agree with Tamzin about Jim and the others; I just thought they were being alarmists too.'

Lindsey was beginning to recover from the queer effects of shock, and thankfully to feel less dream-like. Her cheeks were hot and flushed now, after the coldness of their pallor, and her arm was coming to life with strong and rhythmic throbbings.

She said, 'I'd have done it myself if I'd seen it. And really, I don't think anyone need bother all that much. There'd be the ferry-boat in the morning.'

Mrs Grey's hand slipped down over Lindsey's chair-arm and gently grasped the fingers under the spread coat.

'You bothered about the Lillycrop children, Lindsey!'

'Oh, well –' said Lindsey.

'So we're jolly well going to bother about you!' grinned Rissa.

'Whether you like it or not,' said Meryon, raising one dark eyebrow comically, in the way he had.

'When will they know if the dog has rabies?' Tamzin asked, unable to push down a rising pity for the misery of the dog, no matter what the dire results of its existence, and of her misplaced pity and forgetfulness.

'I don't think we know that,' said the Vicar, characteristically remaining silent about Tamzin's part in the affair. 'He's being very well cared for in the meantime at the Clenches'. But now the urgent problem is getting Lindsey to the doctor. It really ought to be within an hour or two of the bite, I think, but we can't possibly manage that now.'

'Supposing I start at once,' suggested Meryon casually. 'If you think of a quicker way after I've gone, I can easily turn back. But if you don't, time won't have been wasted.'

'Can you really swim two miles?' asked Lindsey, looking at him in frank admiration, and wishing her arm didn't feel so much like red-hot pins and needles.

'I expect so,' said Meryon gallantly. 'Anyway, I can soon find out.' He turned towards the Vicar. 'How about it, sir?'

Tamzin suddenly burst in with, 'I say, I think I've really thought of one – a better idea, I mean. How deep d'you think the water is, Father?'

The Vicar looked at her thoughtfully, for you never could be sure about Tamzin's ideas.

'I expect it varies. Probably anything from two to five or six feet, depending where you are.'

'Well, what I thought was, what about Cascade? He doesn't mind water. Rissa and I have often swum the ponies in the sea. And he could wade wherever it's shallow enough, and swim where it isn't.'

'What, in the dark?' asked Mrs Grey anxiously.

'Of course! How about when we were White Riders? He's used to riding in the dark. In fact you could pretty well say he's quite the perfect pony for the job.'

'And you riding him, I suppose you mean?' Mrs Grey plainly didn't like it.

'Well naturally; he knows me so much better than he does anyone else. And you can't really say it's too dangerous, after all the things we did for the White Cross horses and everything.'*

'You'll get terribly wet,' said Mrs Grey, trying not to fuss. She knew all too well how short was the safety-margin of time for Lindsey before the doctor saw her, if there really was risk of hydrophobia, but Tamzin was her only daughter, and very dearly loved. It wasn't really the getting wet that worried her, either, but the unspoken dangers of the night ride through the waters;

*Told in *Cargo of Horses*.

though she knew that no argument based on danger could have much effect on Tamzin. Or, indeed, on any of these wild young people, she wretchedly reflected. They lived on hazard. Dangerous enterprise was bread-and-butter to them all, except perhaps for Roger, the quiet musical one, but nevertheless he always got himself mixed up in everything the others were engaged in. And now, with the emergency and havoc of the storm, there was no time at all for music . . .

Tamzin was on her feet, the two cats jumping down with injured tail-twitchings to settle on the hearthrug.

'May I borrow your long thigh-boots, Father? They'll keep me drier than my wellingtons, and I'd probably only lose the wellingtons in the water because I shan't have any saddle as the wet would spoil the padding. It won't matter so much about the bridle. I can always soak that in neatsfoot oil when I get back.'

'But, Tamzin –' Mrs Grey felt the ground being snatched from under her feet, as she so often did with Tamzin.

'Mother, *darling*!' Tamzin was itching to be off, and doing something constructive by way of restitution. 'This is no time to talk about wet feet! Come on, be a good mamma and say I can go? You know I'll probably only have to, anyway, because a life's a life, after all, and we can't just sit around and let Lindsey help herself to hydrophobia. And you do see that Cascade can't help getting there miles quicker than Meryon could swim?' She cocked a snook at him, but Meryon's bright blue eyes looked back at her with unfathomable meanings.

'We-ell –' began Mrs Grey uncertainly.

'Oh, *thank* you, Mamariti!' said Tamzin, rushing her fences and using the special pet name she had adopted for her mother. 'It's all right about the thigh-boots, Dad?' She was half-way to the door.

The Vicar valued, above the most fine gold, a spirit of high adventure in the young. Over his precisely joined fingertips he nodded gravely, but the glorious twinkle in his eyes belied the gravity in his voice.

'Certainly, my dear, if your mother is agreeable.'

Tamzin grinned delightedly at Rissa and the boys. She could be cheerful now.

'That's game and set to me!'

'If I had Siani here, it wouldn't be!' Rissa's voice came floating after her, but Tamzin was away down the hall.

'Mrs Briggs, darling! Be a fairy and give me some of that nice fruit cake – a big piece, please – wrapped up in a bit of paper. I'm going to have a night out.'

'You don't say! Sleepin' in the water under the plane trees, I suppose?' Mrs Briggs snorted like an escaped stallion. 'You don't stir a step, me lass, not till I've spoken to your mum, you don't. Fruit cake indeed!' she added indignantly, flopping across the kitchen in the large black plimsolls in which her shapeless feet fitted about as well as crabs in knitting-bags.

But Mrs Grey had already reached the kitchen door and the two of them stood facing each other across the threshold. Mrs Briggs bridled, indignation bristling out of every pore, the firm words struggling silently to the surface of her mind; but Mrs Grey walked in past her with a smile.

'Mrs Briggs dear; Tamzin has offered to ride to Dunsford for the doctor. Lindsey's got rather a nasty dog-bite, and you know the way we're fixed with the boats. I wondered if you'd mind packing a little food for her, in case she's late coming back? I'm going to help her get ready, and the Vicar's writing a note for her to carry to the doctor.'

Mrs Briggs teetered slightly on her plimsolls, looking rather as if she had just been walked through by an apparition.

'Well – since you say so, Mrs Grey love. But no one can't stop a person thinking her own thoughts.' She snapped her pleasant mouth shut firmly, keeping her thoughts where they belonged, and her large feet moved like flippers to the larder.

CHAPTER 13

NIGHT HAZARD

*

TAMZIN wished she had a belt with a torch fastened on to it, such as she had once seen in a shop in Hastings, for the drowned acres of the Marsh were dark as death.

Going up through the village, with her feet barely skimming on the water, it hadn't been so bad: for there the road was higher than it was across the open Marsh, and there were cottages showing lighted windows, and sometimes voices echoing on the water, and these things gave one courage in the darkness.

But now, away past the little church whose roof was built to look like an upturned fishing boat, it all seemed very different. For one thing, it was so much darker; or else it merely seemed so, because she missed the shape of roofs against the sky. And the water began to be so much deeper now; and, instead of her feet skimming and a cheerful splash of Cascade's hoofs in shallow water, there was a swirl and press against her booted legs and only a muffled rippling noise as her pony breasted through the floods.

It was some comfort to know her own green torch was in her pocket, but she felt she oughtn't to use it now, just for company's sake, because she could still make out where the road lay by the dim shapes of telegraph poles beside it. And who could say how much the torch might be needed later, if all did not go well with her on this dark and doubtful journey?

Cascade carried his fine head most high and nobly, like a stallion in a painting. Tamzin knew he did it to

It was darker now, and the water deeper ...
a waste of desolation

keep his muzzle from the water, but the old lyric qualities of her imagination were fired by it, and she was suddenly a Valkyrie, astride a white immortal cloud horse, riding through the towering darkness of the midnight: and the water was the heaviness of thunder-clouds; the distant points of lighted windows were the stars on her own level and, somewhere through unfathomable giddy depths of night, the old world spun below her.

This was a good game, this releasing of a winged imagination like a falcon from a cage, for it took your mind from danger: when the dark water was a legendary storm-cloud, it wasn't any longer a waste of desolation where a drowned sheep might come bumping ghoulishly against your shrinking legs, or where your

pony might suddenly stumble and throw you into
water cold as coffins, black as graves they lie in.

You simply mustn't think of all the pot-holes in the
road, now hidden by the treachery of water.

You mustn't think of those two of the lifeboat crew
who hadn't yet been found. No, please God, not those,
who might be floating . . . floating . . . (What did dead
men look like when they floated in the water? White
and grave and tranquil? Faces staring upwards like
sea-lilies in the darkness? What did it feel like if they
touched against you as you rode, cringing in the
loneliness, so frightened that your heart was rattling
round your ribs in mortal terror?)

You simply mustn't think of drowned men floating . . .

The water was a storm-cloud, and you weren't
Tamzin Grey at all. You were a Valkyrie, wild and fey
and war-like, riding through the stars along un-
charted ways . . .

Dead men floated on the earth, and the earth was
hundreds of light-years away, spinning down in giddy
distances . . .

Now the water swiftly deepened: Cascade lurched,
floundered, leaned his white breast into it; and the lap-
lapping was up above the knees of Tamzin's thigh-
boots.

It was not very easy to imagine at the moment, for
real life was becoming so much more powerful than the
wings of any fancy. Then the movement changed. The
pony was launched, like a little white ship, and was
swimming.

No good now, Tamzin thought, clutching the wet
mane, in remembering how often you had swum
Cascade before. Then was sunlight and sea-sparkle.
Now was darkness and flood-gleam, like cold light seen
on dank well-water, deep inside the earth. Then was

good company and laughter. Now solitude and silence.

The water was inside her thigh-boots, pouring clammily down against her skin, dragging the boots, like sea-anchors, so that she had to hunch her knees up jockey-style to keep them on. The pony swam on, blowing and snorting as the water splashed against his nostrils.

Imagination was very hard to come by, now, when you were so cold and wet, Tamzin thought, and when you were almost sick with that strange blend of fear and boredom which assails you in long-drawn-out danger. She tried to remember how she had felt on previous night hazards, but then there had always been the others with her, and to-night she was more alone than she remembered being ever in her life.

She tried talking to Cascade. But you can't carry on a conversation with a pony who is battling with the water for your sake, and has all that he can manage without flicking back an ear to listen to your chatter.

The minutes went slowly by and still the pony's hoofs had not struck ground. Tamzin began to feel a new fear clutching at her stomach. Supposing the floods were deeper than her father's estimation? Supposing they were deep nearly all the way to Dunsford? How far could Cascade swim? And if he gave out so far from their goal that she should have to turn back – would he find strength to swim home?

Now thoroughly frightened for his sake, as well as for her own, Tamzin slid from his back into the water. For if you were wet up to the waist, she decided, you may as well be wet all over, and she would get warmer swimming by his side as well as making his great burden lighter.

She was careful to keep a vice-like hand-grip on his mane, despite the smarting of her blistered hands inside her gloves, for if they were parted now it might be fatal to them both: she losing all the pony's deep reserves of strength, without which she would soon be overwhelmed beneath the water, and he losing her guiding hand, which kept him from circling over the drowned grazings.

Almost at once she lost her father's thigh-boots, but it simply couldn't be helped, for when you are saving a life you don't count the cost in boots and clothing. Even if she didn't actually lose any more clothing than the socks inside the boots, she had surely spoilt some with soaking in sea-water.

Suddenly, she remembered Mrs Briggs's fruit cake and the buttered scones inside her pocket, regretting them in the absurd way you can regret small things in great emergencies. She was just the same, she thought, as Ariadne, crying for her teddy when her home was filled with water, except that she was twice the age of Ariadne and therefore old enough to know better. But the fruit cake was delectable. And if you have to die, thought Tamzin most dramatically, it is a pity to die hungry . . .

She was now very cold and tired; in fact, she frankly realized, she was exhausted. But Cascade was holding out wonderfully, beating his powerful strokes beneath the water and forging ahead, pulling Tamzin easily alongside. Her right hand gripped tightly in his mane, desperately keeping them together, but the rest of her was so tired that she could hardly think with clearness any more.

How long had they been in deep water? How far along the way were they, by now? Was it half a mile? Less? Or more? Lights were such funny things. You looked at them, twinkling away there in the distance, and you couldn't make up your mind at all as to whether they were still nearly two miles from you, or only half, or a quarter.

She began to wonder, dreamily, whether they would ever come out to shallow water. So tired she was now that she couldn't even bother any longer about the floating sheep and corpses. All she really wanted to do was to leave go and lie back blissfully to sleep, with no more effort. But that, she knew, was madness. You had to keep holding on, keep going, and keep awake; right until the last dram of energy had gone and you couldn't do it any longer. Because you never knew at what moment Cascade's hoofs would strike the bottom, and he would pull himself above the water, and you with him.

Tamzin had become so fuddled with cold and exhaustion that the shape was almost on her before she saw or heard a thing at all. When she did see it, looming well above her, she was so stunned with shock as nearly to let go of Cascade's mane. In that small splinter of a second in which it is possible almost to review a lifetime when confronted with great danger, Tamzin thought of all her family and friends at home, of her pony swimming with her, and of what the shape might be – whether live or dead or supernatural, or just the product of a tired imagination. All this in a fragment out of time. And then it was the voice of Jim Decks in her ears – deliriously welcome, dear, most lovely voice!

'Wodjer hem well think you're thunderin' well doin'? Can't yer see a feller's navigation light? Lord bless us! It's you, is it? Jumping gin bottles! Sink me fer a blockhead, but I might as well er guessed it.'

'Oh, Jim!' She hardly recognized her voice; in fact she hardly heard it, so weak and trembly was it.

'I'll lay you're flaggin' fer a tow, ole young un.

Here, give us a flipper! Cor, darn take it, didjever see the like?'

She might have been an end of cast-off tow-rope, from the ease with which the old man hauled her over the side and dumped her, sagged and soaking, in the bottom of his ferry-boat. But the reins were still clutched firmly in her hand, and Cascade trod the water, snorting, close beside them.

Tamzin had no words. Full of queries, anxieties, and news, she had no strength or breath, this minute, to express them. She just sat there, soggy in the puddle of her dripping, like a blanket lifted from a wash-tub, grasping her pony's reins with all the strength left in her.

Old Jim was likewise silent. He had said his say, and nothing parson's daughter did could shock him now, for long. He just sat down at his oars again, swinging his boat out at an angle to the road.

Tamzin feebly found her voice. 'You're going right off the road, Jim.'

'You got that just a liddle wrong, gal. I'm goin' on it.'

With increasing amazement, Tamzin saw through the darkness her pony rising slowly from the water till it lapped along his flanks and he was standing firm on his four feet, blowing and snorting, his sides panting like a blacksmith's bellows.

'Betcher thought you know'd whur the road was, gal!' Jim was grinning at her. 'Well it ent, see! It's 'ere.'

'Oh, Jim!'

'And you was navigating plumb along the ditch-line. Two strokes from safety, Gawd bless us all!'

'Oh, Jim! I did try so hard to keep straight by the telegraph poles.'

'An' managed, seemingly. Iffen you'd kep' a bit

more crooked you couldn't have stopped yerself from hitting bottom somewheres!'

Tamzin stared at him, feebly taking all this in, but Jim was losing patience, what with the cold and the risks to parson's daughter and her pony, now pitchforked so dramatically into his care. Roughly, he drew his own old navy guernsey round her shoulders, sat down and began to pull steadily for Dunsford, rowing as fast as Cascade could keep up.

'We're a fair spit nearer Dunsford, gal, so you gotter have it, whether you will or no. Nearest port in a shipwreck, as they say, an' I gotter get you rubbed down smartish, see. Towels outside, whisky inside. An' I won't have no back arnswers.'

'It was Dunsford I was going to – for the doctor.'

'Oh, ah.'

The old man went on rowing, calm as vespers. If anyone else were sitting just where I am, thought Tamzin, and looking at old Jim's peaceful face, they'd never guess he wasn't rowing across his ferry. They'd never think, to look at him, that he was rowing over flooded grazings, in the night, with a girl he's just fished up from drowning, and a pony in tow, and never expecting any of it. That's what comes, she thought, of having smugglers in your pedigree. It's just the same with Meryon too, only pirates; the calm way of taking emergencies is just the same with him. I wish, she thought suddenly, remembering her own stark panic about the floating corpses, I wish that I'd had smugglers, instead of lines of famous clergymen. Or perhaps as well as, because a dash of both must make about a perfect character . . .

Aloud, she said, 'No one else but you could pick up a drowning horse and rider, in the middle of the night, and never even ask them why they did it, Jim.'

The ferryman grunted, spitting in his palms.

'There's many a pore codger stands in need of a doctor arter that ole blow,' he said. 'Tent fer me to arsk which one it is this time. Nor not to wonder over who they sent to fetch him, neither, seeing the way I knowed you since you hadn't no front teeth. You mayn't a got overmuch brain, gal – thank the Lord! it's awful in a female – but I will say you got spirit. I said it afore and I says it again: you was wasted on a parsonage. Shoulda bin a sea-faring fambly's child, so you should.'

He spat into the water, rowing onwards.

Tamzin looked at him, astonished. That he should say this, after what she had just been wishing about smugglers and pirates in the ancestry! It was too much, and again she had no words; sitting there, wrapped in Jim Decks's guernsey, holding her pony's reins and trying to stop the chattering of her teeth.

After a few minutes she said, 'Jim, what did Hookey Galley's dog look like? The one he had from a Dutch-man?'

'We-ell, gal, 'twere a tidy great bull-dog type; you know the kind. Drownded now, I'll lay, and good riddance, fer I never saw anything as looked more like going sick, in all me life.'

'Oh, Jim!' Tamzin wound the rein-ends round her salt-sticky fingers. 'Then Lindsey's just been bitten by it! And it was all my fault: I let it into the Institute in the storm. That's what I was going to the doctor for. Oh Jim! How long do people take to die of hydrophobia? Are we going to be in time?'

Jim Decks sniffed comfortably, leaning on his oars.

''Course we are, old young un. Time I wur at school I learned about that Frenchy – him what invented germs – you know –'

'Pasteur?'

'That's the codger. We-ell, he had some chaps brought him what was bit with they mad dogs, see, and one was brought a tedious long time arter, but his ole stuff cured 'em jus' the same. Reckon I prob'ly dis-remember most all they ever taught me, them days, but I call to mind that Frenchy.'

Tamzin sighed with released high tension, her eyes upon the distant lights that suddenly seemed nearer. Perhaps there was still time . . .

She said, 'Jim, I thought you weren't coming home until the morning?'

The ferryman shrugged. 'An' what if I weren't? Can't a feller change his mind?' Then, as a half-regretted afterthought, 'Clatter-clatter-clatter! That's what it is with women. Couldn't never stand it!'

Wrapping herself more closely round in the rough, oil-smelling wool, Tamzin smiled to herself in the darkness.

CHAPTER 14

PLAIN OBSTINACY

*

AT Dunsford, Tamzin and Jim had a series of battles of will, and, as both were people of immense doggedness and determination, they caused each other considerable delay and annoyance.

The old man had tied up his boat at the end of the long Westling road, where the floods ended, and walked with Tamzin on her steaming pony into the ancient town, now cloaked in quietness and darkness.

They were going along the Strand, at the town's foot, when Jim remarked that he thought The Mermaid was the place her father would prefer for her, and that, accordingly, he would now escort her there and see her pony taken to the stable, before going up the High Street to the doctor's house.

'But Jim! I can't possibly stay the night in Dunsford. Father and Mother'd worry themselves to tatters, thinking Cascade and I were both drowned. And in any case, we've simply *got* to find the doctor first. It's a matter of life and death.'

The old man glowered at her, but Tamzin couldn't see this very clearly for the darkness.

'The doctor'll tell yer pa and ma. An' as fer me, I ent a-takin' yew back over them floods ter-night, gal! No, not even if yew wuz to goo down on your bended knees –'

Tamzin snorted, squelching in her sodden clothes upon the sodden pony.

'– bended knees,' repeated Jim firmly. 'I ent a

gooin' to be haunted all me life with letting you knock yerself out with galloping pewmonia. Nor I ent!'

'Oh really, Jim!' said Tamzin, swinging her bare feet in rising irritation. 'As if I were a piece of drawing-room fancy-work! Let's leave all that to argue about later, anyway, because it's simply got to be the doctor first. You must see that. And another few minutes can't do me any harm.'

Determinedly, she turned her pony to the bottom of the long hill, called The Mint, which runs up to the High Street, ignoring absolutely the shadowed foot of cobbled Mermaid Street up which Jim would have ushered her.

Muttering ominously, his white beard wagging, the old man squared himself in front of her, prepared to be ridden over before he let her go another step away from warmth and dryness and safety.

Tamzin's exasperation wavered close to breaking point, so tired she was after this long day of endless strain and struggle.

'I shall just gallop round by Cinque Ports Street,' she warned him.

Old Jim thrust out his tufted chin, standing his ground indomitably, and firmly grasped her bridle.

'It don't take two to fetch a doctor. You'll come along of me or I'll bust taking you.'

'No I won't – not before the doctor's sent to Lindsey. I'll jump down and run barefoot sooner. Oh, Jim! Don't be so block-*headed*! Don't you see I've got to come too? If you take me to The Mermaid now it'll lose us ages, when every minute counts. And if I go alone you know they won't take me in, the way I am, all soaked and everything, and under age, and at this time of night, and no one else to speak for me. And while we're standing here arguing, I'm only getting colder,' she added pathetically, hoping this would touch the old man more than plain obstinacy, of which he had as much as she, in any case.

She won this first sharp tussle, as she later won the next one after the doctor had been despatched in haste to take boat and go to Westling. The next one was about Cascade, whom Tamzin flatly refused to leave in Jim's charge while she was being warmed and dried inside The Mermaid Inn. The old man ranted at her in the stable-yard of the inn, finally forgetting himself so much as to swear at her, though immediately afterwards apologizing for his coloured language. But Tamzin was immovable. If a person owned a pony, it was that person's duty to see the pony properly looked after, she said. In the end she had her way, knowing perfectly well that Jim would probably have treated Cascade just like a boat if left alone with him, sluicing him down with lots of cold water, and other unthinkable seamanlike ideas.

'And besides,' she said humbly, now Jim was seeing reason, 'it does get me so much warmer rubbing him down than it would just rubbing myself down.'

The old ferryman grunted disbelievingly, turning his unaccustomed hand to forking bedding for the pony.

'Jus' like any tarnation farmin' chap,' he grumbled. 'And me a seaman since I give up bibs and pinnies.'

Cascade was soon dry and happily munching at the food provided by the inn – most remarkably provided, Tamzin thought as she finished rubbing round his pasterns, because they could hardly have been expecting a horse to visit them, at such an hour, and in an age of motors. No doubt they had collected it in haste from the man in Traders' Passage who kept a pony for a greengrocery round. She hated to think what the night's adventures were going to cost her father before they were over, but Jim was quite indomitable about not taking her back until the morning, and also about her staying at one of the best of Dunsford's famous inns because ''twadn't seemly in a parson's daughter to be bedded any other how.'

By this time Tamzin was much too tired to argue any more. Jim could easily have bedded her down in the church porch if this should have seemed to him more suitable, for she was past all opposition, and her fighting spirit was already fast asleep.

'Where are you going to spend the night, Jim?' she asked drowsily, as he armed her to the doorway of The Mermaid. 'I suppose 'Stacia'll be asleep by now,' she added, referring to the ferryman's terrifyingly righteous and house-proud wife.

'Oh, ah!' said Jim, nodding sagely in complete agreement. ''Twouldn't never do to stir our 'Stacia outer bed. What I thought,' he said carelessly, 'was of dossin' down alonger your liddle ole pony, see. He keep me warm, gal, and I keep him safe an' comfor'ble, come the mornin' time. Then, when it's still the young of the day, yew git an early brackfuss, gal, and us'll doddle off back home afore the crowds is out, a-starin' at us going.'

Tamzin was far too exhausted to look at the tray-supper brought to her little oak-beamed bedroom in the inn. She gently refused the hot bath that was ready waiting for her, suffered a brief towelling by a sympathetic chamber-maid and was asleep, in a borrowed nightgown, before she was properly tucked in among the hot-water bottles of her longed-for, most desperately needed bed.

The early breakfast was a lost hope, even when Jim Decks had first suggested it, and it was far past 'the young of the day' when Tamzin finally roused herself to tackle the second tray meal offered by her hosts.

'I've never had breakfast in bed in my life before,' she said, somewhat shocked, when the tray was placed in front of her and extra pillows stacked behind. 'Except only when I've been ill, of course,' she added.

The Marsh girl who attended her laughed softly over the pillows.

'It makes a frolic, once in a while or so,' she said kindly.

'Has everyone else had theirs? It must be awfully late.'

'It's turned ten, Miss.'

'Oh, help!' said Tamzin, sprinkling pepper feverishly. 'Jim will be absolutely furious! I say, have you taken him a tray, too? He's in the stable, sleeping with my pony.'

The girl laughed again, incredulously, crossing to the window that overlooked the yard.

'Would that be the gentleman, marching up and down outside the stable? A seaman-like person, with a lot of thick white hair? Oh, my! What would the boss've said! Sleeping in the stable, at the Mermaid! Oh, my!'

'Does he look very cross?' Tamzin swallowed a lump of toast and felt its journey all the way down her throat and through her chest.

'He don't look over joyful, Miss, I will say.'

'Oh dear!' said Tamzin, glancing round the room. 'I say, has anyone dried my clothes, should you think? And – oh – there was some cake and stuff in my coat pocket; spoiled, I expect, with the sea-water, but my pony might enjoy it, if you haven't thrown it away or anything.'

'I'll see about it, Miss. Was there anything else?'

'What, in my pockets, do you mean?'

'No, Miss, anything else you'll be wanting for your breakfast, I meant.'

'Oh, no thanks. Not with Jim marching about like that, and me late, and no one minding the ferry for him or anything.'

'I shouldn't think you need worry about that, Miss,' said the maid comfortingly, pausing at the door. 'From all I hear, I reckon it's pretty well all ferry now, down your way, if you see what I mean. I'll bring your clothes directly, and look, I'll tell you what; I got a nice, warm, old pair of bedsocks and some wore-out slippers what you can have for your poor feet. Bless us, I don't want no thanks! They was put aside for the dustman, but you're welcome.'

When Tamzin did arrive in the stable-yard she certainly presented the sort of sight that had much better get through the town before the folk are all about: her rough-dried coat hung queerly above startling pink socks and blue slippers, and, as she had no brush or comb with her, her long plaits dangled like used hay-wisps, sticky and lank with dried sea-water.

Cascade was clean and shining. 'All ship-shape and Bristol fashion,' as old Jim proudly said, he having groomed the pony most thoroughly with a scrubbing-brush borrowed from a kitchen-maid in exchange for a lucky pebble-with-a-hole-in-it.

The old man's disgruntlement soon vanished with the sight of Tamzin, ready for departure, and after a preliminary grumble about the time of day it was, he threw himself with eagerness and zest to the task of getting under way.

'Soon up anchor and make sail now, gal,' he was saying, handing her the bridle and whistling 'Spanish Ladies' through his teeth. 'I'll betcher feet are middlin' clammy,' he added sympathetically. 'Wind's sharpish, even fer November.'

Tamzin said they were all right, and what a pity it was that she had lost her father's boots. Then she buckled up the throat-lash of the bridle, neatly tucking the strap-end under its keeper before leading the pony out into the yard.

'Here, gimme the halliards!' the old man said helpfully, as she vaulted on to Cascade's back before an astonished and admiring audience at The Mermaid's doors and windows.

'I don't need anyone to hold him, thanks.'

'Please yerself, ole young un. You're skipper on yer own craft,' said Jim obligingly and set off with his straddling sailor's walk beside her. A brief cheer went up from some of the spectators, and Tamzin found herself riotously blushing to her eyebrows, to her intense annoyance, as she clattered out on to the ancient cobbles of Mermaid Street and turned her pony down towards the river and the Strand.

CHAPTER 15

FULLY ILLUSTRATED

*

TAMZIN came running in at the vicarage back door, her slippered feet stiff with cold and her hands full of paper parcels.

'Mother! Mrs Briggs! Here I am! How's Lindsey? Tell me quick – and has the dog got rabies yet?'

'Tamzin, darling! Your poor feet!' Her mother lifted the cats from the windsor chair by the glowing kitchen range where saucepans steamed and bubbled, and drew it closer to the fire.

'What did I say?' demanded Mrs Briggs self-righteously. 'But nobody ever listens to me. Ee, the poor ducks!' she added, melting warmly at the sight of Tamzin's state. 'Now you make her a nice hot cuppa tea, Mrs Grey love, and I'll go and turn the barth on.'

'I don't want tea,' said Tamzin piteously. 'I only want to know about Lindsey and the dog.'

Mrs Grey was kneeling, rubbing the cold feet before the fire.

'Lindsey's all right, darling, and we're almost absolutely sure she'll go on being all right. Doctor Hargreaves gave her the first of a series of inoculations against hydrophobia, and he opened and sterilized the wound itself. He was full of praise for what he called your "heroic journey", because he said every moment's delay would have gone against her chances. But, you know, you're quite a heroine through all the village now, whether you like it or not!'

'Well, I don't much!' Tamzin was always embarrassed by the unaccustomed spotlight of sudden approval, preferring to have neither her bad deeds nor her (less frequent) good deeds brought to public notice. 'Must I have a hot bath, Mamariti? And you haven't said how the dog is? And, look, I've done a lot of shopping for you, but I've had to owe the money.' She thrust the parcels into her mother's lap. 'I made Jim stop and wait a few times, coming from The Mermaid. There's sausages, milk, bloaters, bread, and a *Times*. I thought you mightn't be able to get any of those for a day or two perhaps. And look, we've got headlines in the paper: "Great Gale Sweeps Sussex Coast. Winds Reach Hurricane Force on Romney Marsh. Extensive Damage. Many Lives Feared Lost." And look: "Westling Lifeboat Disaster. Five Dead, Two Missing, From Crew of Seventeen." Oh, Mother! Have they found them yet? Where are Rissa and the boys and everyone? I seem to have been away for ages!'

Mrs Briggs's comfortable voice came trumpeting down the stairs.

'All hot and steamy! Come up and get in it, lovey!'

'Oh dear!' said Tamzin. 'Well, come up with me, Mother! Do! You haven't told me anything at all, yet.'

'I haven't had much chance! Oh well, all right. But I ought to be seeing to the vegetables.'

Up in the bathroom, through mists of steam, scented by the honeysuckle bath-cube that Mrs Briggs's warm heart had led her to extract from the family's small supply (kept for very special occasions), Tamzin and her mother went on exchanging news.

'– but of course we may not know for a few days whether the dog really has rabies; it's just a question of time. In any case, Lindsey's inoculations should be a perfectly adequate protection, since they've been started in such good time – which they wouldn't have been except for you.'

'Oh nonsense, Mother darling! Meryon would have swum. But Mother, do you mean she still really *might* get hydrophobia? Even now?'

Mrs Grey considered. 'Well, I suppose we have to face the fact that she just might. But Doctor Hargreaves is confident she won't.'

Tamzin frowned, turning the hot tap on with one extended foot.

'Mr and Mrs Lillycrop were so overcome by Lindsey's saving all their children,' Mrs Grey went on, washing Tamzin's back as if she had still been a little girl, 'that they sent her a present of a little model schooner, early this morning.'

'Oh, how lovely! I know the one; I've often seen it in their front room. Lucky Lindsey!'

'She thinks so, too. She says she'll keep it for ever and ever, and she's going to call it s.s. *Jupiter*.'

'He was her favourite,' said Tamzin. 'Mind my feet! They're awfully sore underneath. If you'll let me have my flannel I'll go on scrubbing myself. Oh help! My hands are sorer than my feet! Mother darling, d'you think Father'll mind very much about his sea-boots?'

'Of course not, bless you! What a thing to suggest – after all you did to save Lindsey. In any case, you couldn't help it.'

'Oh yes, I could. I mean, it was all because of carelessness. If I'd kept properly on the road I'd never have had to swim at all. Gosh! Now I've lost the soap.'

'I don't suppose you could see *where* you were, in all that darkness. And someone's sure to find them when the water's gone. Tamzin, my dear child, what a mess your hair's in!'

Tamzin found the soap with a quick diving snatch and put it in the soap-tray.

'I know. It'll be agony combing it out.' She was luxuriating in the hot fragrant water, comparing it with the water she had battled with the night before, marvelling to herself that the same simple element could seem so different on two different occasions.

'Out you come!' said her mother, pulling up the bath-plug. But Tamzin lay back, making little waves with her fingers and toes until the water was ebbing down her sides.

'It's so nice to have a bath-cube. Just like before a party or on my birthday.'

'There's Lindsey, coming up with Diccon,' said her mother. 'Hurry up!'

By lunch-time there was no doubt about it at all; Tamzin was beginning influenza, if not worse. Her head ached hotly, her throat was dry, her limbs felt like worn-out bolsters. When her mother had anxiously taken her temperature it was found to be 101, and Tamzin was straightaway hustled into bed with two hot-water bottles, a cold-cure tablet and an aspirin.

Mrs Briggs stumped flat-footedly and devotedly up and down the attic stairs, mothering Tamzin three times as much as Tamzin's own mother thought was good for her, and at the same time chiding her continuously for having got herself wet, for not having dried herself at once, for not having taken the whisky Jim had prescribed for her at The Mermaid – or even a good tot of quinine; in fact, for having gone at all, when she, Mrs Briggs, had been so firmly set against it. With all this, however, Mrs Briggs was not the woman to omit the proper homage due to a heroine, and she toiled up the stairs again with a vase full of paper flowers she had lovingly made from Christmas wrapping paper (there being no real flowers, or even leaves, anywhere on the Marsh since the gale), with fruit drinks and puzzles, extra pillows, magazines, and both the vicarage cats.

Lindsey and Diccon were only allowed to look round the edge of the door for a few minutes once or twice, because of catching the infection and because Lindsey had to avoid all unnecessary exertion while having her course of inoculations. Meryon and Roger and Rissa were not allowed even this much, because of over-exciting the patient. But they wrote a series of fully illustrated notes, which they sent up by Mrs Briggs, telling Tamzin all about the morning's work of salvage in the village and Harbour, and asking her about her night in Dunsford. The notes continued up the attic stairs throughout the day.

Have not forgotten to feed cats, but cannot till you send them down with Mrs Briggs. Love, Rissa. P.S. *Do they have it cold or warm?*

'Here, give 'em to me, ducks!' said Mrs Briggs, on handing in this note, which was profusely illustrated with back views of variegated cats. 'I read it while I got me breath on the landing,' she explained quite unashamedly.

Great news! Just heard from Charlie Briggs (who came in for Mrs B. to dress his thumb) that one of the two missing men is alive and well at Dymchurch. Not Billy Gudgeon, unfortunately (I mean because he was the youngest) but the other one. I don't know his name, but Mrs B. will tell you all. Yours, Meryon.

As Meryon had thought, so Mrs Briggs did. She was telling Tamzin all about it (plumping up her pillows as she did so) all the time Tamzin was reading the note. It was, of course, young Truggy Upjohn, she explained: a wonderful swimmer (which was surprising enough in a Westling man and accounted for his coming ashore so far from home), and what her Char had told her was that poor Truggy had washed up as one dead, and without a stitch of clothes. And of course the shepherd

A temperature and influenza,
if not worse

who had found him, beyond Dymchurch, hadn't heard a word of the lifeboat disaster (what with the telephones being out of order and everything) and didn't know from Adam who he was. And when he'd fetched him round to consciousness again he was so excited he gave him rather too much whisky, and (being on an empty stomach) it knocked the poor man right out again till past midnight, when it was too late to do anything at all until the morning.

'Oh well,' said Tamzin, fumbling for her handkerchief under four or five piled-up pillows, 'it's barvellous they've fowd hib, ad I dare say the extra sleep was the best possible thig for hib.'

A faintly sinister tone was struck by the last sentence in a note from Roger.

Do you want anything? If so, you've only to say and we'll get it: though how anybody can get anything at all in these parts until the flood's gone down is more than I can say, but if anybody can, we will.

There's some talk of a boat coming down from Dunsford with provisions in the evening. If so, she may have empty places going back. Yours, Roger.

This note was ringed round with minute drawings of every conceivable thing that Tamzin might possibly fancy, from a pair of elephants with young, to a desert island with a palm-tree in the middle.

There was a long gap in the afternoon when no notes came up the attic stairs. Tamzin was told that everyone had gone out again to help with salvage operations, except for Lindsey who had to rest, and that she herself was to sleep in quietness until tea-time.

The cats were brought up again and settled purring on her eiderdown. The pillows were reduced in number and Tamzin tried to go to sleep. It was no use, of course, for it was broad daylight and her head ached too much, and her nose was so stuffy that she had to keep blowing it. In any case, how could anyone sleep who was surrounded by the sea where no sea ought to be, and whose mind was whirled around by storm-tossed lifeboats, mad dogs, floating corpses, drunk survivors, night hazards and vanished cottages?

She thought a lot about the old, far-off days when the sea had been over the whole of Romney Marsh, right up to the long line of inland cliffs, and how, during all the years when it had slowly been receding, Sussex folk had always said, 'You mark my words! The sea will always come back to its own.'

Well, now it had done so, Tamzin thought. It had come right back in a night; back over the grazings, drowning the sheep and cattle; back round the cottages, filling cellars and kitchens with brackish scummy water; back over the gardens, covering the winter vegetables. Now, from her high south window, no river was to be seen any more: only the flood water, wide and dark and glittering, with sea-gulls drawing their endless patterns across the sky above it. Tamzin felt as if she were lying in the cabin of a ship – an old-fashioned ship that had windows instead of portholes – for wherever she looked, to north or south, the water stretched around her.

It was, of course, quite futile to think of going to sleep, she said to herself, wondering whether it would be a very mutinous thing to reach across for those extra pillows piled on the chair beside her and to sit up to finish writing that note to Rissa about what to do with the ponies for the night.

In view of all this, it was utterly amazing that, a little later, she had to be awoken from deep slumber by her mother with a tea-tray and another folded note.

'It seems such a pity to wake you, darling, but I do think you wouldn't have a very good night if I left you to sleep on longer, now. Rissa's sent you another note – they've just come in – and Mrs Briggs has made you some tomato sandwiches, and boiled you an egg. How are you feeling now, after your sleep?'

'Oh, all right I think, thank you. Oh, jubpig gid

bottles! By doze is such a duisadse!' Tamzin blew it loudly, several times. 'That's better! Fancy me going to sleep! And just when I was thinking I never would be able to.'

Mrs Grey plumped back the extra pillows and put the cats outside the door because of the tea-tray. She drew the curtains and lit the little oil-lamp, because the room was growing dark, and told Tamzin all about how the Unknown Man's identity had now been finally established as that of a Dutchman, Frans Steen, missing from a coastal barge in the river.

Tamzin sipped her hot lemon-and-honey, staring over the top of it at Mrs Briggs's sandwiches (so beautifully thin, and with their crusts off: how she would have loved them at any other time!) and at Rissa's note, which she was saving for company when her mother had gone down.

'Will he be sent back to Holland, then?' she asked. 'Or buried here?'

'Oh, here in Westling, with the others; unless there's too much water in the churchyard.'

'What a very stately thing!' said Tamzin gravely. 'An eight-fold burial. I hope I'm better in time for it. And I hope that doesn't sound awful,' she added hastily. 'I know how sad and solemn it is. I only meant, it's one of those things that don't often happen in a lifetime – like earthquakes and Halley's Comet – and when they do, it's rather a pity to miss them.'

'I see what you mean,' said Mrs Grey, tidying up a jig-saw puzzle. 'But isn't it rather a good thing? That they hardly come once in a lifetime, I mean! If that's a note for downstairs that you're writing, I'll take it with me, shall I?'

'Oh yes, thanks! It's for Rissa, all about how to do

the ponies. Though I expect she thinks she knows. It's finished now.'

Tamzin folded it up and saw it leave the attic before she settled to her tea and Rissa's note to her.

Just come in. Marvellous afternoon helping old Jim repair the damage to young Jimmy's fishing smack. We've done the ponies, too. And just in case you think they aren't done properly (as you will), they are.

Have you heard the Unknown isn't Unknown any more? He's a Dutchman off a barge.

Provision boat expected from Dunsford any time. We're told to be prepared for taking empty places! Think of school *to-morrow, after all we've just lived through! Love, Rissa.*

P.S. – *Can I come up for ten minutes or so and catch your flu? Or could you send me something you've just breathed on?*

There were a lot of fearful illustrations of germs and bacilli, and a sad little drawing of two boys and a girl sailing away towards the sunset in a boat marked 'Provisions', and there was a P.P.S. in Meryon's handwriting which said:

Don't be a gump! It takes a day to incubate. Ask any doctor.

Tamzin screwed up the note, stared sorrowfully at Mrs Briggs's sandwiches and pushed the tray right down to the bottom of her bed.

CHAPTER 16

GALLANT SPIRIT

*

THE last days of November hung round Tamzin's neck like a weighted rope, after all the high excitement crammed in one short week-end. She was recurrently ill, and she was worried by the unaccustomed burden of anxiety on Lindsey's account, for not only did she have the simple fear for Lindsey that was shared by so many (especially Lindsey's own family who wrote and telephoned daily) but she had also the sickening awareness that the accident had been all her own fault.

It was encouraging that Hookey's bulldog (still under observation at the Institute) had shown no further signs of illness and was, indeed, reported as having much improved spirits and appetite. Doctor Hargreaves took an increasingly optimistic view; he was, he told Mrs Grey, as much worried about Tamzin, whose influenza (after a temporary recovery) had relapsed suddenly into a catarrhal patch on her left lung.

'She's so rarely ill,' he had said, 'but with this she seems to have very little natural resistance.'

And so it was that after only three days up, Tamzin was back in bed again and having M. & B. tablets every six hours, night and day, feeling depressed and dull and worried (all characteristics utterly foreign to her), and being bored, but without the energy to do anything much to occupy herself.

The floods had gone down enough to permit almost normal road traffic and the joy of regular daily posts again, but though Tamzin received frequent letters from Meryon, Roger, and Rissa – long since back at school – she found herself unable to make the effort to answer them.

Lindsey remained at the vicarage; partly for continuity of her anti-hydrophobia treatment, and partly as company for Tamzin, Doctor Hargreaves having suggested that what Tamzin really needed was to be encouraged to renew her old interest in things and to take a strong determined grasp on life.

Lindsey was not made unwell by the injections and she spent hours with Tamzin in her room, reading to her, persuading her to play halma or draughts or snakes and ladders, or just sitting quietly if Tamzin obviously wanted this. She kept her in touch with all the local news of receding flood, returned refugees, repaired and reopened cottages and the like, and, earlier in Tamzin's illness, of the great eight-fold burial which had, miraculously, been achieved in the little churchyard despite unthinkable difficulties of digging in the midst of wide flood-water.

'There were two men digging and two baling out all the time, because the water soaked in as fast as the earth and shingle were dug out. The whole thing had to be baled out again just before the funeral. And Tamzin, the grave was nearly as big as Jim's ferry hut.'

Then, on the day of the funeral itself: 'You simply wouldn't believe the crowds that were there! Scores of men from different lifeboat crews, and from the London offices too. And nearly all Dunsford and Winklesea, I should say. And there were newspaper men, and men with film cameras – one climbed right up to the top of a telegraph pole, Tamzin, to film the coffins passing up the village in the boats. But you could hardly see the coffins at all for wreaths and flowers, the Dutchman's just the same. The lifeboat ones were covered with

Union Jacks, and there were only two words on them, besides the names.'

'Mm?'

'It said, "Died Gallantly".'

'Well, they did,' said Tamzin. 'What a pity that they never found Billy Gudgeon.'

'Jim Decks says it's because he went overboard first. He must have drifted away on a different current from the one that carried the others in to the shore. But if you look out of your south window when the tide turns, you'll see the *Samphire* going down the river, carrying wreaths for him. They're going to throw them on to the sea, just where the lifeboat capsized.'

Long after all the piled flowers of the great funeral had faded, Tamzin was still in bed.

'The lung itself is clear enough now,' said the doctor, 'but the child just doesn't seem to be able to make a full recovery. The M. & B., of course, might have had a depressing effect, but now she is no longer having it she still seems very low. You don't imagine she is worrying about anything, I suppose?'

Mrs Grey shook her head. 'I don't see what she *can* be worrying about, besides the anxiety for Lindsey. She asked me again this morning whether I was sure there was no cure for hydrophobia and that people getting it always died. When shall we know for certain that Lindsey's out of any danger?'

The doctor took a notebook from his pocket, turning the leaves.

'I should say, about December the 7th. But, in any case, there really is practically no danger at all, you know. We were very prompt with the first injection, thanks to Tamzin, and that makes a great deal of difference to Lindsey's chances.'

'But even a very slight risk,' said Mrs Grey, frowning a little, 'might make her worry, don't you think? I mean, Lindsey is her friend, on a visit to her house. I suppose she realizes it would never have happened at all, except for her. You know, Tamzin may seem practical and sensible, but she has a tremendous imagination. And, being as ill as she has been, I suppose it all seems much more serious to her than it might have done if she'd been well.'

'I wonder,' said the doctor, 'if you could get her away for a holiday, somewhere? Not a very good time of year for it, I know, but it might just do the trick – to get her away from the atmosphere of flood and disaster and funerals and hydrophobia and the rest.'

Mrs Grey said doubtfully, 'Well, yes, I suppose we could, of course. But I don't think it would be any good till Lindsey's treatment is finished.' Suddenly she glanced at Doctor Hargreaves with grave remorseful eyes. 'You know, I do feel it's all been my fault, Doctor. I must have been mad to let her go. Meryon wanted to, and he's made of so much tougher stuff. But Tamzin's idea of taking her pony seemed more sensible than Meryon's swimming, and, well, Richard and I have always tried not to spoil her spirit of adventure. It seemed to us a precious thing in anyone, in this too-civilized age – the zest to take risks in high adventure for great and noble causes.'

Doctor Hargreaves shook his head. 'You are all wrong, of course! Wrong to blame yourself, I mean. But you are right in valuing so highly a gallant spirit, such as Tamzin's. You can't imagine how inspiring it is to one sickened by the daily sight of modern young people, queueing outside cinemas – yes, even on the loveliest summer evenings of the year. Don't, Gwenda my dear, don't be the one to clip her wings. You know,

I've sometimes thought of Tamzin and those three friends of hers as belonging to the sixteenth century, born out of their time into our humdrum age. How that young Fairbrass would have loved to sail with Raleigh!'

'I don't know about Tamzin and Rissa, though,' said Mrs Grey, smiling. 'They would have hated those long skirts! If they were to be happy in those days, they'd have had to be boys.'

'Don't you believe it!' said the doctor, picking up his bag. 'If they can be so enterprising in the twentieth century, there'd be no holding them down in any age – especially with such wise parents as they mostly have now!'

Mrs Briggs was untiring in her efforts to make tasty and appetizing dishes for the invalid Tamzin, and for Lindsey in her suspenseful time of waiting. She would toil into Dunsford on her afternoons off, just to get ice-cream and out-of-season fruit with which to make wonderful many-coloured sundaes in tall glasses. She would make milk-cocoa, chilling it quickly outside in the sharp November air, and then would whip it up till it was frothy as spindrift, topping it with cream saved from the morning's milk, or with ice-cream if she had just returned from Dunsford, and taking it up to Tamzin's room with transparent straws through which the rich brown liquid could be seen rising from the foam, like a delicious waterspout rising from a spumy chocolate sea.

Jim Decks too was a frequent visitor, which said a great deal for his loyalty to Tamzin, for he always felt he needed to have a good tidy-up before entering the vicarage, and old Jim hated being really clean and brushed and tidy even more than he hated being ill himself. He brought ends of ropes and a marline-spike, to teach her new knots and splicing; he brought a hunk of sycamore wood and his own most treasured scalping-knife (brought back from a long-ago deep-sea voyage) with which to tempt her to try her hand at carving a little model schooner like Lindsey's s.s. *Jupiter*.

Lindsey would gladly have given the *Jupiter* to Tamzin, dearly as she loved it herself, but Tamzin wouldn't hear of such a thing. And still she didn't seem to have the energy to let Jim help her make one for herself. Sometimes the old man would sit whittling at the lump of sycamore himself, just to give her the initiative to carry on. The curled shavings drifted on to her bedroom floor like white crumpled leaves, and he would go down stiffly on to his knees before he left and pick up each one, stuffing them down into his pockets all among the black plug tobacco, the string and matches and old clay-pipe ends.

'Don't you lose almost everything else when you turn out those shavings, Jim?' Tamzin once asked him. 'Why don't you bring a little bag, or something?'

'What! Me, with a liddle ole bag?'

Once or twice Lindsey's parents had motored over to see her and to consult with Doctor Hargreaves, bearing presents of farm produce and admirably concealing the anxiety which they must have felt acutely. Lindsey herself was well aware of the black remorse and self-condemnation that overwhelmed Tamzin anew whenever these visits happened, and she would strive to make her happier by saying, 'You know, Mother said last night she thought you were one of the bravest people she had ever met, riding through the floods the way you did, in blackest darkness,' or, 'Father was saying anyone with any decency would've let a dog in from a storm like that one,' or, 'The vet is pretty sure now that Hookey's dog is all right after all.' But it wasn't any good. Tamzin was held down firmly in the combined grip of illness, anxiety and remorse.

Lindsey would bring all the heartening news of receding flood, repaired and reopened cottages, new vicarage windows, returned refugees and drained grazings, but Tamzin would only say half-heartedly how she wished she could get up and do something to help, but the strength was not in her.

At week-ends, Rissa and the boys would come down to Westling, bringing all kinds of things to amuse Tamzin. Roger brought a book called *Cats' Cradles From Many Lands*, and a piece of string tied to just the right length for Tamzin to try the figures in the book.

'They'll keep your fingers supple for when you get up and start practising your violin again.'

Meryon brought a morse-code buzzer so that she could send messages to people downstairs.

'Not that anyone minds the least bit, I should think, coming up to see what you want; but it'll keep you awfully well up in your morse, and you'll be so fast at it, when you get up, that none of us will be able to keep pace with you.'

Rissa brought a most expensive-looking thick, stiff-backed exercise book and three pencils.

'Because you always used to say you never had time to write all the stories you kept on thinking out, what with school and homework and the ponies and everything. Well, now you *have* the time, I thought the implements might start you off. You never know what masterpieces you might be brewing in your mind.'

But Mrs Briggs, dusting in Tamzin's room one morning early in December, noticed sadly how the dust lay on the morse-code buzzer, *Cats' Cradles From Many Lands,* the exercise book, and the hunk of half-shaped sycamore.

CHAPTER 17

OPERATION SANTA CLAUS

*

WITH the coming of the second week in December, came the joyful certainty that Lindsey could not have hydrophobia. The relief felt by everyone who knew about it was so great that, on the day of the doctor's final visit and good news, the whole village burst out into a day of celebration.

All the Lillycrop children marched down to the vicarage front door, two by two, carrying tiny posies of violets which must have cost their mother a little fortune up in Dunsford.

Jim Decks stuck a small flag in the handlebars of his old tricycle and pedalled up and down in front of the vicarage, blowing a whistle, before coming in to offer his congratulations and to announce that the slow wheels of the law had at last caught up with Hookey Galley, who had been fined a large sum for evading the quarantine regulations. But it would have taken much more than this piece of news to dampen the high spirits in the vicarage, and no one spared Hookey even the tribute of one sad thought.

Mrs Briggs made a grand and festive cake, with feather-icing and Lindsey's name all over it, except in a few places where she put Tamzin's too, because, she said, Tamzin was a heroine as well.

Rissa and Roger and Meryon all telephoned during the day to hear the news, and there was a wonderful greetings telegram for Lindsey from her Surrey farmhouse home, and after that another one to say there were some parcels in the post.

Even Smiling Morn the grocer came out of his habitual despondency to bring gifts of chocolates and six coloured balloons with squeaks in them, and to say that his grown-up son out in Canada was much more impressed by the story of Lindsey and the mad dog than he was with all the news of the hurricane and the flood.

Diccon brought in endless bits of old leafage and twigs and grasses, which had survived the great storm, to decorate the vicarage hall and stairs, but when his mother found they mostly harboured snails she had them all taken down again for a full inspection before they were allowed to go back.

So gay and festive was the whole place, in fact, that it was well into the evening before Mrs Grey suddenly began to realize that Tamzin had, for the first time in weeks, seemed really her old self again. She had, now, been up and about more or less as usual for some days, but her slow convalescence had not satisfied the doctor, and her mother had been feeling frankly worried.

But on this great day, when no longer need one wonder how it felt to die of hydrophobia, Tamzin had been almost as gay as anyone else. She had slid down the banisters, Mrs Grey reflected happily as she washed the supper dishes; she had played at being an elephant for Diccon; she had practised on her violin for the first time since her illness, and, above all, she had eaten everything so heartily that even Mrs Briggs was stirred to thankful prayer.

'You know what it was about that dog,' Lindsey said happily to Tamzin. 'It was just a straightforward case of homesickness and exposure. Changing masters like that, and countries too, and I don't suppose Hookey was the very best of masters and then being left out in all that hurricane and everything.'

Tamzin nodded. 'I expect Hookey beat him, really, and that was why he *was* out in the storm. I must say I hope he doesn't have to go back to Hookey now. Father says Albert Clench got very fond of him, looking after him all that time, and he hoped he'd be able to keep him.'

And as the week passed it was plain to everyone; the day of Lindsey's release from danger had been the day when Tamzin's full recovery had started. Whether the thing that had held her back for so long had really been anxiety for Lindsey, Mrs Grey decided she might never know. She wondered whether Tamzin even knew, herself; for you can worry a great deal in the far-back corners of your mind and never fully realize how great the worry is.

However, the only thing that really mattered was that Tamzin was herself again; shouting and laughing all over the house, wildly untidy in her room ('At least,' thought Mrs Grey, despairingly surveying the glorious muddle, 'it's nice to know she wouldn't do it unless she really were feeling well!') and never having time enough in any day for all the things she wanted to do in it.

There was to be no more school, the doctor said, until after the Christmas holidays, for the term was so nearly over already. And Lindsey's holiday visit had been extended to cover Christmas, because so much had happened to spoil the first part.

'Only a few days before everyone breaks up!' Tamzin said joyfully. 'And then there's a whole month to do everything we want in!'

These few days turned out to be quite crowded ones for Tamzin and Lindsey, who, shocked by the amount of storm damage still so plainly evident in the village, dedicated all their free hours to working for the restoration of familiar homes and gardens. Cascade and his trap were freely used for carting stored furniture and other treasures from the Mission Hall and vicarage, inns, and higher cottages where they had so long been stored, back to the dried and cleaned-out homes where they belonged.

Even Diccon would sometimes help with tidying shattered gardens (a task that could often end in glorious bonfires), holding Cascade at cottage doorways, or running errands to Smiling Morn's or the post office. Tamzin and Lindsey tackled everything, from scrubbing kitchen floors and cleaning windows, to baby-minding in the afternoons or sewing up new curtains in the evenings.

They were also soon drawn into a whole new field of quite delightful activity because of a fund the Vicar had been organizing for Christmas presents for all the children related to the victims of the storm. The fund had had great popular appeal, and more than fifty pounds had been received at the vicarage since the disaster for this purpose alone, besides the thousands that had been sent by sympathetic people all over the world for pensions for the dependants.

'Fifty pounds to spend on toys for children! Think of it, Gwenda,' said the Vicar to his wife one evening as they worked together over the accounts of the Disaster Fund. 'What do you think we'd better do with it?'

'Why, buy toys with it, of course,' said Mrs Grey sensibly.

'I'm not sure,' said the Vicar, 'that I feel capable of choosing toys for so many different children of so many different ages. What, for example, does a little girl of four want most of all for Christmas? And what about the babies? And the toddlers? I think,' he added after a moment, 'you had really better tackle this yourself, you know.'

'Oh, but I haven't anything like the time to spare for spending fifty pounds in toy-shops, Richard! It would mean at least a whole day in Hastings, and so near Christmas, too. I couldn't possibly!'

'Don't be absurd, dear,' said the Vicar affectionately. 'You always find time for the essentials.'

Mrs Grey suddenly looked up over her ledger with an idea in her eyes. 'I've got a much better notion than that!'

'You have?'

'Why not let Tamzin and Lindsey do it? And Diccon too: he'd be a great help in choosing for the little boys. And, after all, who can possibly know better what the young really want than the young themselves?'

The Vicar pondered the matter a moment. 'You don't think fifty pounds rather a lot for them to handle? Rather a responsibility?'

Mrs Grey laughed. 'Of course not! They'd adore it, too. Ask any child how it would like to spend fifty pounds in a day on toys alone – even for other children.'

'I think it must be *more* fun spending it on other children,' said the Vicar characteristically.

'Well, there you are then! We needn't give them the money, of course. We can phone the shops first, before they go, and arrange about the approximate sums to be spent, and they can all be paid by cheque after the toys have been delivered.'

Mrs Grey opened the ledger at a blank page near the back.

'I think the first thing would be to make a list of all the related children, don't you? In fact I do really think it ought to be all the children in the village, irrespective of whether they're related, because there can't be many who aren't, and fifty pounds is a very great deal of money.'

'There are forty-seven children in the village under school-leaving age. Yes, I think we should include them all,' said the Vicar, warming to the idea. 'It will work out to a pound for each child and a little over for any odd sixpences on prices.'

Mrs Grey was filling her fountain-pen with royal-blue ink.

'What a wonderful time Tamzin and Lindsey and Diccon are going to have! I almost envy them enough to wish I had the time for it, myself. Now, I've finished these accounts, so I'll use this spare page for the children. We'd better start with the Lillycrops, as they're related to practically everyone.'

'Did you know,' said the Vicar, looking up over his glasses, 'that they've decided at last on names for those new twins?'

'Oh dear!' said Mrs Grey. 'Have they? I hope they're not too Lillycroppian; it's awful to think of the poor little things having to grow up with such labels.'

'They could be worse, I suppose. The choice is Samson and Delilah. Mrs Lillycrop said she was sure I would be specially pleased because the names were Biblical.'

'Oh dear!' said Mrs Grey. 'Oh well, as you say, they could possibly have been worse. I'd better put them first on my list, as they're quite the youngest children in the village . . .'

And so one of the first things Tamzin did, after her recovery was considered to be complete, was to set off after an early breakfast with Lindsey and Diccon for Hastings, carrying a list of forty-seven names in her pocket and enough money for a really grand lunch and tea for the three of them, because the whole of the long day would obviously be required for such a large-scale Santa Claus operation as theirs was.

It was wonderful that the weather was so good – a crisp and sparkly winter's morning such as makes the blood run swifter – but even the worst of weather could hardly have taken the magic from the morning, because, as Lindsey said, the thrill of Christmas shopping is a thing you carry inside yourself.

Diccon was enchanted at the prospect of acting Father Christmas on such a spectacular scale, and if he did feel twinges at times because nothing at all was meant for him he kept them bravely to himself.

The train journey, to begin with, was exciting enough to three who hardly ever travelled in a train. There were the strange exciting smells of the station, and the clanking, bumping noises of shunting trains, of luggage, and of milk-cans; all so clear and ringing to the ears because of the sharpness of the morning.

In the train, there was the eager interest in other local passengers, faces vaguely familiar to Tamzin but not known as you know the people of your own village. A man with baskets of fish, two smart women who probably worked in Hastings offices, and a mother with a baby, and a push-chair which Tamzin helped to fold and lift into the carriage.

There was the growing excitement of counting off the little halts; Snailham, Doleham, and Three Oaks, before the noisier arrival into Oare, and, finally, the glorious whistling and panting slide into Hastings, the little engine getting its breath with long hissing sighs of steam while Tamzin, Lindsey, and Diccon tumbled out of their carriage and raced along the platform for the stairs.

Down Havelock Road they went and round into broad Robertson Street, sniffing the oddness of petrol smells, fish-shop smells, vegetable and grocery and bakery smells, straight to the first of the shops on their list.

Tamzin made Diccon hold her hand when crossing the busy street, and though he felt this was a little degrading in a six-year-old he wouldn't allow his pride to spoil the morning. After all, wasn't he going to act Father Christmas to more than a dozen other children? And that was enough for any boy's pride to be getting on with, thought Diccon, diving into the doorway of the toy-shop two leaps ahead of Tamzin and Lindsey.

The toy-rooms were upstairs. In fact, with sports-room and hobbies-room they covered the entire first floor of the building, and, at this early hour of the day, Tamzin's party found them almost deserted, except for a few isolated very early shoppers.

The whole place was lavishly decorated for Christmas, with paper-chains, holly, mistletoe, and ivy, and silver bells. Down at the far end was a towering frosted Christmas tree, as hung with toys and baubles as the holly was with scarlet berries. Everywhere you looked were toys, and more toys. They were stacked in tiers on shelves right up to the ceiling, all among the tinsel and the paper-chains; they were piled on tables down the middle of the rooms; crowded on benches round the sides and – the bigger toys, such as tricycles and sledges – herded together in every possible place upon the floor. The colour of them all together was so uproarious that it almost shouted at you, and Tamzin and Lindsey stood in the doorway with Diccon for a brief half-minute to get accustomed to the dazzle and the riot.

Diccon was not so helpful as everyone had hoped

Then Diccon bolted down the room. He had seen the grand display of electric trains, switched on already for the early shoppers and running round the intricately laid-out track through little towns and villages, past a fully-stocked farm, through tunnels and stations, and under bridges. There were signals that really worked from a distant switch, and there were goods yards and engine-sheds and level-crossings – everything to scale.

'Well!' said Tamzin, coming to earth next. 'Perhaps we'd better find an assistant, and make a start somewhere. Though where on earth to start in all this –'

'Who's first on the list?'

'Samson and Delilah.' Tamzin grinned, walking down between the crowded toys as through a forest. 'They're six months old. What on earth do they play with at that age?'

The morning in the toy-shop passed like fifteen minutes, so absorbing, difficult, and fascinating was their task. The assistant they found to help them was quite useful with good ideas, such as buying Christmas labels to tie on each toy with the name of the child for whom the toy was chosen, and packing smaller oddments around toys whose price was lower than the average. But Diccon was not so helpful as everyone had hoped, until, after a full hour of gloating over it, he had thoroughly worked the electric railway out of his system and finally accepted the fact that they couldn't spend the whole fifty pounds on one grand complete railway set, to be laid out on the billiard-table in the Sailors' Institute and worked by himself for the joy of all the village children.

'Now listen, Dicky,' Tamzin was saying. 'Lindsey and I've done more than a quarter of the list, and you haven't helped at all. We've left all the children of about your age, and now's your last chance to choose for them.'

'Well, if you really think we can't *possibly* do the railway –' began Diccon, staring at it regretfully over a half-turned shoulder.

'You *know* we can't,' Tamzin interrupted, trying not to spoil the morning with sudden exasperation. 'It has to be one separate present each, and not to cost more than twenty shillings and sixpence. Who's the first one of the names we left for Diccon, Lindsey?'

'Hydrangea Lillycrop,' said Lindsey, studying the list. 'Then three more Lillycrops: Jupiter, Ariadne, and Cleopatra. We've done Samson and Delilah, with those baby-swings for doorways.'

From this moment Diccon pushed the railway from his mind, and suddenly became so useful that they wondered how they could possibly have managed without him.

'Oh, I know just what Jupiter would love!'

'He's only four-and-a-half,' Tamzin reminded him, 'if you were thinking of Meccano.'

'I wasn't. I was thinking of one of those big lorries – there! You can steer them properly with the wheel, and you can go fast or slow, or in reverse. And the tail-board goes down, as well as the whole wagon part tipping if you want. Look, I'll show you!'

The assistant placed one of the fleet of lorries on to the ground and, while Diccon demonstrated its points, Lindsey put a tick on the list by Jupiter's name and wrote 'mechanical lorry' beside it. Tamzin chose a Christmas label with a robin on it and wrote in capital letters: 'HAPPY CHRISTMAS TO JU', resting the label on a shelf among a crowd of china dolls as she wrote.

'Why not "Jupiter"?' asked Lindsey. 'Shortenings are so ugly.'

'He's used to it,' said Tamzin, tying the label to the scarlet-painted steering-wheel, 'so it'll make it seem more homely.'

Diccon was rubbing his chin reflectively, standing close to the soaring Christmas tree.

'I just don't know about girls. All the other Lillycrops are girls, till you get to Ur, and he must be quite ten or so. Have you chosen something for him?'

'I don't believe we have,' said Lindsey, running a finger down the list. 'No, we haven't.'

'Good,' said Diccon. 'What he wants most is a telescope. I heard him say so, round the Point once.'

'Can you get a telescope for a pound?' Tamzin queried.

The assistant leaned attentively sideways.

'Oh yes, madam! We have several very nice ones from eleven-and-six. This way, please!'

Tamzin was writing 'HAPPY CHRISTMAS UR', on another label balanced on her palm, as she slowly followed the others down between the coloured banks of toys.

By half past twelve, when Lindsey suggested a break for lunch before the cafés got too crowded, they had done more than half their list, so full of inspiration had Diccon been. Not once had his eyes strayed back to the splendid array of the electric railway, and round him they swiftly gathered boxes of building bricks, and Meccano; a little set of Sussex trug baskets with trowel, spade, and fork; fishing rods, cameras, Tyrolean dolls, and clockwork railway sets; horse and carts, scooters, and aeroplanes; a dolls' house, a garage with three cars in it, and a crimson-painted wheelbarrow,

complete with a little green watering-can inside it to
make up the price to twenty shillings.

Despite what he had said about the girls, he seemed
to have the right ideas for every age, boys and girls
alike; and he noticed things, such as the cameras, that
Tamzin and Lindsey had completely overlooked in
making their earlier purchases.

Such a writing of names and a tying-on of labels
there had been.

When they were out in the cold air of the crowded
street again Tamzin felt quite queer, as if she were
suddenly stepping into a different land; so long had
they been clustered round with toys and brilliant
Christmas decorations. You had to focus your eyes all
differently out of doors, and the colour had gone clean
away from everything, or so it seemed, in contrast to
the toy-rooms.

They found a café down the street, where Tamzin
knew a friendly ginger cat, and they even found a table
by the window where they could look out on the unaccustomed sights of daily life in town. Diccon was
enraptured, his ordinary days being even more soaked
in village life than were the older children's.

'Oh, I *say*! That man with a little cart – he's actually
sweeping up the *street*! Wouldn't Mrs Briggs laugh!'

And, 'Quick Tamzin and Lindsey! Do look; a
shopping basket on *wheels*!'

'Yes, we know, Dicky darling. What do you want for
your lunch? You can choose anything on this list, down
to here. Not from the bottom bit because all those are
frightfully expensive, and though Mother did say we
could have a grand lunch, she can't really have meant
as grand as that.'

'I know what I want. Fish and chips. The square-
oblong kind, not the round ones.'

'But you haven't even looked at the menu!' Tamzin said.

'I know. I don't much care for strange food. I like something I know the taste of, in case I might choose something horrid.'

Lindsey passed the menu card across to Tamzin.

'Oh, let him have them, then. They're on the list. I think I'm having the same, because we never have chips at home, and never fish in batter.'

'Crisp and brown!' said Diccon, nodding in agreement.

'Well, we do,' said Tamzin, staring at the card. 'It's Mrs Briggs's special. They'd never do them here the same as she does.'

A waitress came and stood beside their table, the ginger cat at her heels. Lindsey and Diccon swooped lovingly on the cat at the same time and Tamzin looked up saying, 'Two fish-and-chips, please –'

'The square-oblong kind!' Diccon added. 'Oh, and could we have water with *ice* in it?' He made a gesture signifying ice.

'With ice in? Certainly, sir!' The waitress smiled and Diccon goggled, scarcely believing his ears.

'Sh! Diccon. And one chicken salad, please!' continued Tamzin. 'I always like them, even in the winter,' she added to Lindsey.

'I know,' said Lindsey, 'the way one does ice-cream. I say, I do hope those twenty-shilling cameras will be all right. They're awfully cheap for cameras.'

'I expect they will,' said Tamzin, looking around at the other customers. 'They're pretty strong. I do think the telescopes were an awfully good idea: I didn't know you could get toy ones.'

'Oh, *look*!' said Diccon ecstatically, clutching the ginger cat upon his knee as he leaned to gaze through the window. 'A double-seater pram with twins in it! Wouldn't Mrs Lillycrop love that for Samson and Delilah?'

Although there was now less than half the list to finish, it took the whole of a long afternoon to accomplish it, for there were several shops to visit, including a bookshop for some of the more bookish children. There was also the enormous excitement of discovering a second-hand twin push-chair in front of a shop in Queen's Road, and recklessly deciding to risk the very reasonable price of twenty-one-and-six upon it for Samson and Delilah.

'Because you can see we shall have quite that much over, when we've finished,' Lindsey said.

'And Mrs Lillycrop would be so thrilled with it!' said Tamzin.

'Just as I said in the café!' said Diccon, jumping round it. 'I *said* how she'd love a twin push-chair!'

It was quite dark before the last name was ticked and the last label written and tied. Then there was more rapture for Diccon in walking out from the bookshop into a miraculously darkened and lit-up street, with rows of glittering decorated windows, and great pearls of light hung dazzlingly overhead like floating moons.

'Oh, I *say*! And it was quite light when we went into the bookshop! Oh, wait a minute –' He hung back, pulling Tamzin's hand. 'This window's full of strings of fairy-lights! Do *look*!'

Tamzin hesitated, glancing at the clocks in a watchmaker's next to the fairy-lights. 'Golly! The time!'

'Well anyway, we've finished,' said Lindsey happily. 'And we have had fun!'

'How Rissa and Roger would have loved it all! Even Meryon, perhaps. Yes, Diccon, they're marvellous, aren't they? Tea now, old chap; creambuns if you like. Anything on the menu this time.'

Turning away from the lights with a sigh of brimming contentment, Diccon followed, threading dreamily through the Christmas crowds.

'And then the train again!' he said blissfully. 'That will be lit-up, too!'

CHAPTER 18

MANY LANTERNS

*

Long before Christmas Eve the parcels had arrived. So many there were that the small spare room was specially reserved for them, and there they waited, stacked on chairs, bed, window-sill and floor, until the Great Day dawned.

Tamzin and Lindsey and Diccon had spent hours in this room, wrapping up the smaller things in festive paper, covered all over with holly and little fir trees and children on toboggans, and the bigger things in strong brown paper which they tied with coloured string and decorated with little Christmas stamps, and bright green Christmas trees done with Tamzin's water-colours or Diccon's birthday crayons.

Even after everything was done that anyone could think of – the last piece of holly-paper used and the last stamp stuck – the three of them would sometimes look inside the room at all the glory of piled-up parcels, thinking of Christmas morning and how Margaret would like her camera, Robert his fishing-rod, or little Jupiter his lorry. The twin push-chair – now beautifully cleaned and shiny, with its handles wrapped round and round in green crêpe-paper – had almost a benevolent look, wheel-deep in presents, and with its vast seat buried under parcels.

Through these last days before Christmas there was also the excitement of the carol-singing practices. Rissa and the boys were down at Westling nearly every day for long hours of riding, rowing and sailing, staying late into the dark evenings for singing with the choir at the church. Tamzin was not a regular member of the choir, much as she would have liked to be, for her father said it was better to have as many as possible helping to swell the tiny congregations. But at Christmas-time she and Rissa and the boys had always joined in for the carol-singing practices and for those memorable Christmas Eve outings when they sang to all the village, trudging round the lanes and tracks with swinging lanterns in their hands.

This Christmas Eve the carol singing was not the only highlight, nor even the most exciting one, for after it was over would come the second part of Operation Santa Claus, when all the chosen toys would be delivered at the doors of sleeping children.

Tamzin was thinking of this as she walked among the other singers down the Hard to their first stopping place upon the little wooden quay.

'Just to think of the weather staying so crisp and marvellous!' she said, drawing deep cold breaths of the night-sparkling air as their feet crunched briskly over the shingle.

Roger said, 'Snow would have been better,' tucking his fiddle-case closer under his arm for climbing the fence between the shingle and the quay.

'Not for the toys afterwards,' Tamzin said. 'Unless it was a very little snow, because of Cascade and the ponycart.'

'Not even better for the singing, really,' said Lindsey, 'because voices carry better on a clear frosty night.'

The dark boards of the quay rang under their feet and the many lanterns bobbed and swung along with them, surrounding them with hazy spheres of light. There was no moon, but the stars were brilliant in the frost and the tall masts in the Harbour stood out like charcoal drawings on the sky.

Roger was tuning his fiddle and a man with an accordion blew upon his fingers.

'Jolly good thing you practised harder since the summer,' Tamzin said to Roger.

'Quiet, everybody,' said Charlie Deeprose the choirmaster. 'We will start with *The First Nowell*.'

He raised his hand, and round him the circle of faces, white in the lantern-light, watched for his signal to begin.

Down came the choirmaster's hand and up soared the first phrases, like white wings in the darkness of the night, rising into the stars' ways and swooping to the sliding glimmer of the river as it glided past the quay.

Tamzin's heart went up with the wings of the carol, for music was to her – as Lindsey had said of Christmas shopping – a thing she carried inside herself. Roger too was concerned only with the pattern they were making in the winter air, as you could see by the faraway expression on his face above the tilt of his violin. But for Meryon and Rissa and Lindsey the singing was only a part of the magic of the evening. They would always remember it as much for the exhilarating cold of it; the brightness of the stars and blackness of the water; the lantern-light and friendliness, and the mince-pies, ginger-beer and coffee that would welcome them at many cottages that night.

They sang beneath the Harbour Mast, its white yards and rigging shining in the light from their lanterns like a mast of the fated Flying Dutchman.

They sang at the Deeproses' Harbour Farm, where they were brought inside the warm kitchen for the cocoa, cakes and pies that old Mrs Deeprose's lavish hand pressed on them, though only slowly was the farm building up again after all its devastation and loss.

Old Mr Deeprose asked the Vicar, before the carol singers left, to offer a prayer of thankfulness for the deliverance of the village from the floods. And when one remembered the completeness of the havoc Harbour Farm had suffered (its flocks and dairy herd lost, its grazings ruined by salt-water) it was not easy to listen without a lump inside the throat.

Then on to the Sailors' Institute they went, where Roger's fingers failed him so for cold that he had reluctantly to put away his fiddle for a time and play his mouth organ instead.

The lanterns bobbed away up the village lighting up the flood-marks on the walls, the broken trees and the gardens wrecked by water. They were going to the Sea Serpent Inn, for the Vicar believed in carrying Christianity into all unlikely places, and here they sang inside the bar-parlour and afterwards there was beer and cider for the older ones, and soft drinks for the younger ones; all 'on the house', with more mince-pies, and also shortbreads, apple tarts, and chocolate marshmallows.

'Not another thing for me! Not till to-morrow dinner-time,' said Tamzin, from the depths of her great full-ness, as they went out again into the darkness and the frost.

They sang down at the low cluster of the Coast-guards' Cottages, at the Schoolhouse near the church, and then far away out at Shepherd Smeed's and Shep-herd Tewmell's lonely cottages, where still the flood-water lay in isolated gleams upon the Marsh. Last of all, and doubly welcome to tired feet and voices, was the Merrows' Castle Farm. Away beyond ruined Cloudesley Castle and built from its great fallen stones, the farmhouse stood like a citadel of homeliness in miles of lonely grazings. Thatched and beetle-browed, it was the centre of all comfort for man and beast. Its ruling spirit was Mrs Merrow herself; she who never turned away even the roughest tinker without rest and food and drink ('For you never know when you may be entertaining an angel unawares'), who had adopted, as her own son, Jonah, the young, swearing, tobacco-chewing beer-drinker of unknown sea-faring origin ('For I allus wanted a large fambly, and it's wunnerful what you can do with simple loving-kindness, good food and proper home life') and who cooked like the arch-angel Gabriel but with the plentiful hand of Bacchus. ('There's nothing like a lot of what you fancy for doing you good.') Mrs Merrow had more than the choir would have believed possible in view of the flood disaster, of all the nicest Christmas foods and drinks, and it was a pity, Meryon said (letting his belt out a hole), that they hadn't had the sense to sing at her place first.

'We'd never have got any farther if we had!' grinned Rissa, finding room for yet another mince-pie, to her own astonishment.

Jonah – long since renamed Joseph – handed the piled plates round the seated choristers for all the world like any other farmer's son who had never known a life of kicks and crime and sudden danger.

Mr Merrow got out his own old fiddle, dreamily tuning it below the hanging oil-lamp in the window, and, after the last inch of room had been found for the last delectable little pie, a new wave of singing broke from the Westling choir, in Mrs Merrow's wide old sitting-room, among the sheep-dogs and the cats, the old crooked beams and yellow-shining oil-lamps, the driftwood fire and hanging holly branches.

Very late it was when all were home again. Tamzin and Roger yawned and yawned in ecstasies of weariness, but no one would have dreamed of suggesting they should miss the final part of Operation Santa Claus.

Now the lanterns swung towards the vicarage stable, and noises came from there of clinking buckles, bit and curb-chain, and of iron shoes upon the yard-stones. Tamzin brought her pony-trap around to the front door, close against the doorstep, and out from the vicarage began the coming-and-going procession of the carriers of toys. First the vast twin-seater push-chair, rustling in its swathings of green crêpe-paper, then the steady-flowing river of decorated parcels, pouring from the vicarage front door and coming to rest, like a little coloured pool, in the deep dam of Cascade's tub-cart.

'I hope we've packed everything in order,' Meryon was saying doubtfully, as a corner, down beside the fishing-rods and stilts, was found for the last small parcel. 'We want to avoid a lot of coming and going, if we're to get this mountain all delivered before the morning.'

'It's nearly the morning now,' said Rissa, peering at her watch.

'I thought it must be,' said Tamzin, yawning again. 'Here we go, then: Operation Santa Claus, Act Two!'

Cascade leaned into his collar with a willing burst of energy ('It's all very well for him!' said Tamzin, 'He's been standing in his stable all the evening') and Roger and Meryon rushed ahead to open the double gates.

Tamzin, at the bridle, led the wonderful load out safely to the dark deserted roadway, the others crowding after.

'We're like smugglers! We only want masks and

muffled wheels,' said Roger, finding sudden stores of
vigour.

'No,' said Tamzin, walking swiftly by her pony's
head. 'Not on Christmas Eve, and with a load of toys
higher than our heads. What we really ought to have is
bells, and a sleigh with a great carved prow, and sixteen
reindeer pulling it!'

'And the sky for a road!' said Lindsey, lifting expressive arms.

'And more toys,' said Meryon, smiling, 'than all the
children in the world.'

'It *is* the morning, now!' said Rissa suddenly.
'Happy Christmas, everyone! Happy Christmas!'

'Well it is!' said Roger. 'Already!'

Down Westling village street the sound of hoofs came
clear and ringing in the frosty air: and if sleeping
children, half-hearing it in dreams, thought they heard
the passing of the reindeer, who can say they were so
far away from truth?